The Delphi Room

MELIA McCLURE

FIRST EDITION

The Delphi Room © 2013 by Melia McClure
Cover artwork © 2013 by Erik Mohr
Cover design © 2013 by Samantha Beiko
Interior design © 2013 by Danny Evarts

Distributed in Canada by
HarperCollins Canada Ltd.
1995 Markham Road
Scarborough, ON M1B 5M8
Toll Free: 1-800-387-0117
e-mail: hcorder@harpercollins.com

Distributed in the U.S. by
Diamond Book Distributors
1966 Greenspring Drive
Timonium, MD 21093
Phone: 1-410-560-7100 x826
e-mail: books@diamondbookdistributors.com

Library and Archives Canada Cataloguing in Publication

McClure, Melia, 1979-, author
The delphi room / Melia McClure.

Issued in print and electronic formats.
ISBN 978-1-77148-185-4 (pbk.)
ISBN 978-1-77148-186-1 (pdf)

I. Title.

PS8625.C584D44 2013 C813'.6 C2013-903948-1
C2013-903949-X

CHIZINE PUBLICATIONS
Toronto, Canada
www.chizinepub.com
info@chizinepub.com

Edited by Samantha Beiko
Proofread by Klaudia Bednarczyk

We acknowledge the support of the Canada Council for the Arts which last year invested $20.1 million in writing and publishing throughout Canada.

Published with the generous assistance of the Ontario Arts Council.

Printed in Canada

For my parents, Patrick and Jacqueline,
and my sisters, Kara and Chelsi,
with infinite love and gratitude

and

For Scott,
in his memory

THE DELPHI ROOM

I

My mother was on her way over the day I hung myself. Only I didn't know it, because she never calls in advance. I never intended for her to find me, but at the time I wasn't thinking about who would. The bathroom tiles needed re-grouting; mildew stains spread like grubby wings. I had bought some grout—it still sat under the bathroom sink behind a collection of bright pink razors and an explosion of make-up. Pieces of the ceiling had crumbled away, exposing the pipes—should've had that fixed, too. Doyenne of domesticity, I am not.

My mother had let herself in as usual. (How did she get a key? Is her doppelganger a locksmith?) I think she brought some chicken soup and some leftover chow mein. (A combination guaranteed to cure any cold—I had spoken to her a couple of days before and complained of a sore throat.) She talked as she came through the door, calling out to me and commenting, true to form, on the weather/traffic/state of my abode, eyes sharp to the ruin or repair. (Mostly—this time—ruin.) She left her shoes—marvellous shoes, Italian leather always, *(like buttah!)*, purchased on Commercial Drive—at the foot of the hat stand. I never actually kept any hats on it, but I have always been rather taken with the jauntiness of hat stands. (You could imagine one coming to life and having a winning personality, singing and dancing and with the voice of Liza Minnelli.) In the kitchen she set down her C&C cold cure, as she calls it, commenting all the while, I'm sure, on the stacks of dishes in the sink, Pyrex plates with satiny layers of congealed foodstuffs in various earthy colourations.

I hadn't done the dishes in two weeks. I hadn't eaten in three days. There was nothing left to eat on, and anyway I hadn't gone grocery shopping. If I did it again, I would make the effort and do a little Martha Stewart-ing. Prepare the tomb, like an Egyptian slave. Then nobody could say the girl was nuts *and* she didn't have clean underwear.

My mother must have panicked right away when she didn't hear my voice. She has always been the dramatic type, and though she is full-bodied and loud-voiced, I have always thought of her as an enamelled butterfly whose lacquer is just about to crack. I must have been dangling several minutes by then, limp as a dishrag, sallow skin overtaken by an icy blue like twilight. The fan was whirring in the bathroom; I had turned it on earlier because my CD player was broken and I couldn't stand the sound of the silence. I didn't want to hear music anyway, didn't want to hear the honeyed smoke of anyone's voice timbre-ing up and down some sweet scherzo. I wanted blankness. I wanted white noise. The bathroom fan was the closest I could get to it—the steady, unfaltering, noisy noiseless noise.

Peregrinations all night long: bare feet on the floorboards and the tick of the clock, punctuation for my pacing. Hair a rope of grease, goose bumps bubble-wrapping my arms. Night-shod, The Drive was eerily quiet: no traffic-ruckus hemp-and-muslin bustle drifted down toward my door. Streetlight melted through my curtains. I was not crying.

In the kitchen I wet a sponge so I could stamp my bills—I don't like the taste of the glue. There were several: phone, cable, credit cards. I was usually late with my bills, but not this time. I wiped the crumbs from the kitchen table and stacked and re-stacked the envelopes, settling with cable on top.

Several bottles of pills sat on the counter. I had not taken any in three months. (Or was it four?) I'm not sure why I'd hung on to them, except that looking at the bottles kind of felt like sleeping with a security blanket. But all comfort had disappeared, and become unnecessary. So I gathered up the bottles and threw them in the garbage.

The sun started to appear, blue-ing the big black dome of sky. I went into the bathroom, turned on the bathtub faucet and plugged the drain. Upstairs a toilet flushed and I stared at the pipes in the ceiling, imagining the goods in transit. On the edge of the tub sat a bottle of pale yellow oil. I poured the whole thing in. Beside that sat a bag of fizzy bath bursts, sherbet-hued and floral-scented, and I added those as well. Then from the cupboard beneath the sink, I pulled a large basket of round soft bath beads, bright and perfect like plastic jewels with secret, liquid hearts. I stood at the edge of the tub and dropped them into the water one by one, and watched the liquid without release the liquid within. Tea lights were scattered around the bathtub and across the counter, and I picked up my butane lighter and sparked them with slow ceremonial flourish. Once upon a time bathing was a ritual, a spiritual act—I had never liked showers. It was always much more satisfying to see the ring of grime after a bath, and feel lighter, having left something behind. After my candles were lit I turned off the faucet. The trapped water nudged at the edge of the tub, as though trying to see over. I undressed slowly: off came chartreuse-trimmed fitted black pants, beaded pink top, big white country-girl underwear (my own private protest against the assault of the G-string) and a once cream-coloured bra that I had accidentally dyed pistachio-pudding-green in the wash. I lowered myself in slowly, careful not to let any of the water slosh on my tea lights. I lay on the bottom, head underwater, and looked up. The perfumed water assaulted my eyes, but the sting was somehow distant, a pain from the past. The remains of the bath beads floated overhead: melted stars, fruit-toned lily pads. I blew bubbles to swirl them, then watched them go still and sat up, disturbing the surface of the water very slowly—first the top of my head, then my eyes, nose, and mouth. I leaned back and drew the bath bead bodies closer, capping each finger with a dissolving half-orb. Stretching my fingers out in front of me, I inspected my handiwork: grotesque nail polish. Tea light wax grew clear, gave the appearance of flame leaping from water. Candles' hot gold hearts licked and swam, an audience—breathless, charged up, responsive. I put my hands beneath the surface, watched my lacquer melt free of my fingertips, leaned back and closed my eyes. There was a pulsing just behind the lids, a steady, resigned, ludicrous heartbeat. I lay like that for quite a while, a soak of sweat beading my face, breathing in the combustion of competing scents rising from the water.

INT. VELVET'S BATHROOM—EARLY MORNING

A young woman named Velvet lies in her bathtub, twisting and untwisting her pubic hair. The Shadowman sits on a stool beside her. He is middle-aged, handsome, and dressed in black cashmere.

SHADOWMAN

Will you go forth today? Shall I put on some Billie Holiday? Does the "Lady Sing the Blues"?

VELVET

Why do you like jazz so much?

SHADOWMAN

Music of the soul, my friend. God plays the trumpet. And today, Velvet, God's playin' it for you.

Velvet starts to cry. She rips out a clump of her pubic hair. There is blood.

SHADOWMAN

Tsk, tsk. Now look what you've done. Save it for your crossing.

Velvet looks at him in horror.

SHADOWMAN

Just kidding. Clean, like I told you.

I heaved myself out of the tub; the water had chilled and I shivered, though the hairs on my upper lip were encased in tiny sweat-sarcophagi. I watched the tub swallow its contents down the drain, studied the dark slime-gritty ring, saw the bits of gel-smeary bath bead shells dotting the bottom like sticky confetti. Head hung over the sink, I slurped cold water, splashed my face. The mirror gave myself back to me, cruel in its faithfulness. My nose breathed the heavy, flowery air. I patted my face and body on a dirty pink towel and retrieved my make-up bag from the cupboard. I wanted to wear my new red lipstick. Out came foundations (semi-matte, matte, pancake), powders (pressed, loose, iridescent), blush (gel, crème, powder), glosses (sparkly and non), tints, eyebrow brushes, eyelash combs, mascaras (brown, black, purple), shadows (creaseproof and waterproof) and liners (liquid and pencil): palette arsenal, compact theatrics. White lotion glopped into the palm of my hand, smeared over my face, sank down pores. I found the red I was after, still in its box. Eyes in the glass looked out at me: remote, slow blinkers. A blitz of powder, cornsilky grains speckled with sparkles. Audrey Hepburn channels Bambi: doe-eye black liquid liner taking flight at the corners. Petal-pink cheeks, hibiscus tint with a soft, soft finish. My special lipstick I uncapped and turned up as far as it would go—a true '40s coming-in-on-a-wing-and-a-prayer red, glam, glam. I put it on thick, venturing a little beyond my natural borders.

INT. VELVET'S BATHROOM—MORNING

Velvet applies her make-up with great care, although her hands are shaking. The Shadowman stands behind her, inspecting her reflection.

SHADOWMAN

That's it, darling—blend, blend, blend! I adore bold colours, they remind me of the Moulin Rouge.

Velvet is crying again.

SHADOWMAN

For fuck's sake, they won't let you into Heaven with raccoon eyes!

Perfume next. Vanilla base, spicy top note, cut with sandalwood. I drenched myself with it, watched strands of scent lengthen down my chest, disappear under my breasts.

Barber's scissors lay on the edge of the sink.

INT. VELVET'S BATHROOM—MORNING

The Shadowman runs his fingers through Velvet's hair.

SHADOWMAN

A trim, darling, just a trim.

He wraps his hands around her throat. Their eyes meet in the mirror. He smiles. Her gaze glitters with fear.

I dragged my fingers through my hair trying to unclump it, spools of wet threads wound tight. My hair was long, ends sprinkling water on my lower back. I started at the front. Winding the end of one wooly whorl around my index finger, I picked up the scissors and began to trim the spray of splits that shot off. At first, meticulous; then hacking, wielding my scissors with abandon, the way I did once upon a time, when I scalped Barbie before stirring a tub of Dep with her head. Locks fell dead and heavy, inert half-curls. I sliced away at the back of my neck, coming around my left cheek with a flourish, then hedgeclippered some bangs, a thick forehead curtain. Stuck-her-finger-in-a-socket Louise Brooks. Smoothed down the bobbed frizz with pineapple-scented serum, looked long at my exposed shoulders, collarbone emptying to a hollow at the base of my throat.

Hairs stuck to the bottoms of my feet and then shed onto the hardwood floor as I walked to the bedroom. Clothes on my bed, on the floor, on my chair. Morning light passing a note through the blinds gave the room a movie theatre feel, lush-jet of brilliance in the darkness.

INT. VELVET'S BEDROOM—MORNING

The Shadowman stands beside the closet, leaning languidly against the wall. He is dressed in full drag queen regalia, complete with red wig, four-inch patent leather stilettos and fishnet stockings. He starts to sing a song from *Kiss of the Spider Woman*—"Dressing Them Up." After a few bars, he pauses, pulls out a nail file and begins to file his long red fake nails. He stares at Velvet, his mouth contorted by a vicious smirk.

SHADOWMAN

It's about time you got the fuck out of here, you little whore. 'Course, I'd really rather burn you alive, but I—

VELVET

(screams)

Shut up Shut up Shut up! I can't think I can't think let me think!

The Shadowman whips off his stiletto heel and starts to pummel Velvet in the face. Her lip splits and lacerations, like angry fault lines, crack open, oozing blood.

I stood at my closet, fingering sleeves, skirts, buttons. Face to a 1920 lace shawl, spider web on my cheek. Velvet pants (in honour of my name) with ankles swelling to soft bells. A white halter dress sweetened with tiny cherries, worn with Sabrina heels and a sense of great expectation. Next to that, the one I wanted, circa 1938 cut on the bias, lip-red, gem-sparkly. I took it out of the closet and laid it on my bed. From a bureau drawer I removed a black satiny bra. Wired myself in and then slipped the dress off the hanger and stepped inside, pulling it up slowly, chiffon column rising from the red puddle at my ankles. At the foot of the bed: orange and yellow chicken slippers, black satin heels. I chose the evening shoes, buckled up. Moved to the vanity mirror, added small pearl drop earrings. I was a silvery photograph, the watery light in the room gathering handfuls of dress, grey-red sepia cast, my eyes dulled and dusty as the bottom of a trunk. High up in the elm in the front yard, the lonely, straggling note of a bird clung to the morning breeze.

On a hook in my closet hung my favourite belt: silvery, lizard-skin, '70s. I picked it up, rubbing the roughness of the miniscule geometric pattern on the skin. I walked to the bathroom, slowly and with even, deliberate—regal—steps, trailing the hem of my dress, long belt and perfume behind me. The humidity had dissipated, but the cloying sweetness of my bath remained. On the inside of the tub the dirty ring had darkened and dried to a peeling horizon. My pink towel lay on the floor and I picked it up, scrunching the fibres in my fist.

I hung it over the mirror.

I pressed my lips together.

I tasted my lipstick.

I smelled my perfume.

I smoothed my hips.

I straightened my spine.

I climbed onto the toilet.
I tied the belt to the pipes.
I belted my neck.
I breathed in and out.

And then—

My mother set the food down on the kitchen counter, shook her head at the mess and called my name with particular emphasis on the first syllable.

Vel-*vet. Are you in the bathroom?*

I imagine I swayed, a tiny gesture, difficult to see.

Honey? Are you still asleep? You're supposed to be at—

She entered the bathroom and her voice tangled and then slip-knotted in her throat, fraying to a scream. Up, up, up went the pitch and bang, bang, bang went the door, Mr. Cassidy from upstairs interjecting his plump fist into my mother's wails. She was trying to un-belt my neck, he was opening the door, calling out, moving into the hall.

I was whizzing headfirst down a slide, in the dark.

Mr. Cassidy got me free while my mother sucked air and salt from the tears that were running over her lips. He yelled at her to find the phone, pressed his mouth to my Joan Crawford red. The phone wasn't in plain sight; I remember that. I had stuffed it under two Chinese embroidered pillows to muffle the sound.

In the place where I had gone it was still dark, though I was on my feet, walking, with Mr. Cassidy's breath rushing at my heels like the charge of air in a SkyTrain station when the train is threading itself into the eye of the terminal.

My mother found the phone jack and tracked the cord to the phone, picked up the receiver and blanked. She couldn't remember her name or my address. Mr. Cassidy shouted information over the whir of the fan. Clippings of my hair from the floor were sticking to my skin and my dress. My skin was less blue, more rice powder.

In a while, the plaintive chide of a siren sliced the morning on my street. I had always wanted to ride in an ambulance. They get more attention than limousines or hearses, and anyway, if you're riding in a hearse you hardly get to appreciate it. As it turned out, though, I was still bumping around in the dark place, unaware of the red-dressed body

I had left behind, so I never got to experience the noble hovering of the paramedics above me as they tried to get my dust-bag lungs to pump. Dreams never happen quite the way you hope.

Up ahead, faint auras of light sharpened as I neared. The glow was sucked back into the yellow hearts of streetlamps carving rows of doors out of the shadow. Each door was white and large, taller than average, and heavy looking. All of the knobs were gold. I stopped walking and stared for a long time, waiting for God to throw out a lightning bolt or something.

In the ambulance my mother and Mr. Cassidy crowded beside me. My dress was twisted and there was a welt on my neck. New bob frizzy, as though I'd dropped a toaster in the bath instead. My mother squeezed my hand until it matched my dress and the man in uniform monitored and fussed, trying to revive Ophelia.

No lightning bolts, or fireworks, no river to cross or gate to pass through, no guest book to sign. No one offering to film a single memory to keep, like in a movie I saw (I knew that couldn't be true), no signs, no fare to pay. It was like being stood up on a blind date, except you can't call the friend who set you up and ream her out.

Mr. Cassidy bit his fingernails. My mother said my name over and over.

I chose a door.

The siren shrilled on.

I opened it.

My mother sobbed.

I stepped inside.

Velvet, Velvet, Velvet, Velvet, Velvet, Velvet—

2

The heavy door shut behind me with surprising force, as if pushed from the other side. Vast vistas of cloud-tinged azure? No, a small room with blush pink walls and a frilly coconut pie of a bed. The lighting was florescent and over-bright. I moved to the bed and touched the bedspread, a delicate eyelet with matching pillow shams, the kind I begged my mother to buy me when I was ten. How our tastes change. Over the bed was a barred window, which at first I thought had a white blind over it, until I put my fingertips to the glass, felt the coolness and realized that the whiteness beyond was the view. Stuffed animals sat on the eyelet and on the deep windowsill, tattered and well-loved, ones I recognized: Paddington Bear with hat and raincoat, black and yellow bumblebee with mesh wings, chocolate brown dog with large ears muffing its head and a very tattered, rather small almond-coloured bear—Beary Bear—with a fraying nose. They had all belonged to me. A gilt-edged mirror hung beside the bed, a built-in picture of cherubs above the glass. It was then that I saw: no red dress, no fancy shoes. Just flesh. (Why wasn't I cold? I thought, this place must have central heating.) I looked thinner, although mirrors can be deceiving. What to do when you find yourself unexpectedly naked? I climbed into bed.

Okay. What the Hell? I drew the pink sheets up under my chin. On the opposite side of the room was a beautiful Chinese screen traced with the fine lines of bamboo leaves. On one side of it was a small writing desk on which sat a yellow legal pad and a purple gel pen. In front of the desk sat a matching chair. On the other side of the screen was a closet, and on the wall next to it was a clock that was stopped at 8:57. I got out of bed and approached the closet, panic playing a calliope behind my ribs. The door opened and inside was a childish pink sundress, simple sheath, to the knee. Thank God—I ripped it off the hanger, shimmied in. And that's when I thought—there must be some mistake. I turned to the room's big white door, seized the gold knob and yanked—yanked—yanked, but the door remained closed.

Breathe. That's what I told myself. So I stood there for a few moments, sucking oxygen and shaking like a wet cat, before I quit dignity and started pounding on the door. Surely God wasn't deaf. What had I hoped God would say to me at the pearly gates? I don't know . . . You're better looking in person? I wasn't sure, but I thought there'd be something, some form of dialogue. Who's minding the store, here? This couldn't be the inn Christina Rossetti was referring to; the poem didn't say one word about being trapped. But you can only shriek for so long before you start to feel ridiculous—even in this place, apparently, self-consciousness lives—and besides that, my voice started to shrivel to a croak. So either God had eyeshades on and earplugs in, or I was being ignored. Either way, I felt like tearing out Paddington Bear's stuffing and writhing on the floor like an overturned crab.

I went to the bed and settled for hurling poor Paddington at the door, causing his little rain hat to fly off. I sprawled out on the eyelet and stared at the ceiling, which I now noticed, to my further chagrin, was covered with glow-in-the-dark suns and moons and stars, just like the ones I'd had and loved, until they stopped glowing and refused to recharge, no matter how much time I spent shining a flashlight on them. Ambushed by my childhood. Surprised there wasn't a TV playing nonstop *Scooby-Doo*. So I lay there, tracing the outlines of perfect stars with an imaginary finger, whirlpooled by confusion. And disappointment. And rage. And then horror, as I felt the familiar cold sluice of despair.

After a while—who knows how long, there were no real suns and moons and stars to guide me—I realized I was scrunching the eyelet so hard my fists ached, tears waterfalling into the thicket of my bob. I had always been a person who believed in signs, and the appalling lack of them was terrifying. It was becoming evident that no Big Hand was going to pluck me clear through the stick-on solar system—room service was even doubtful. Not that I was hungry, appetite had gone the way of my life. But I was frantic to hear the rap of another being on the other side of the door: Welcome Velvet, glad you could join us. Or maybe the lack of signs was the sign; this is it kid, this is what all the do-gooding (okay, well, maybe "good intentions" would be more accurate) is for. But no, the stuffed animals, all the childhood hauntings, must be ushering me back through the annals of my life, preparing to spit me out fresh the other side. Then, the thought that had been jostling all the others buffaloed to the front of the line: I hung myself, now Eternity is going to hang me out to dry. Through all of the heart-mash, nerve-searing sadness and terror of the Shadowman, I'd never believed in Hell—a depressed optimist? Was this the brutal serves-you-right-you-should-have-known-better Truth? I'd always loved to be alone, no one imposing on my aura, pricking my energy field. The quiet shoaling into the chattery crevices of my mind. Alone was a kind of Heaven, if that word can be used to describe anything on Earth. But this was a prison, and even worse than that, I was still the same, steel-boxed inside the Hell in my head. (Though the Shadowman hadn't shown up yet, threatening to burn me alive—so maybe my wish had come true and I'd escaped.) But solitary forever? I expected people who liked me, people I liked. Falling into open arms as if into a womb of fleece.

Well, wasn't this a Welcome Home party. Break out the charred hors d'oeuvres. Where was the giant spit to roast myself on?

And that's when I thought of Purgatory. The med-doped, middling mood, or non-mood, the thick-aired, sludgy-boned half-state. Was I in a waiting room, being voted on, before being passed on to The Dentist with the Eternal Drill, or a champagne-clinking First Supper with well-padded chairs and chocolate soufflé?

Neurons ricocheted, limbs accordioned in. I lay on my side embryo-tight, and screamed. Screamed. Screamed. Screamed until I curdled, decibel-spent, on the floor. And then there I was, sweat, tears (blood? I can do that too—where's my razor?), ears throbbing, bulldozed by stasis.

I got up, lurching, staggering through timeless Void, and faced the seraphim-festooned mirror. Red lips gone. Winged Hepburn liner gone. Face parchment-plain, dark almost black eyes headlighting out of the pale. I could see the bob might've been a good idea if it'd been cut with a steady hand, with a few layers shredded in, but now it looked like an electrified headdress. Oh well, no heads to turn. I looked as wan and waxy as I had in the weeks before I'd turned myself into a mobile, or, correction, before I'd covered the mess of my face with my string-up makeover. Mirror shone back the self I remembered, although it seemed the checkerboard of tendons had started to loosen, once pearl-round cheeks flattening into a small, drooping mouth. Eyelids puffy from crying, new awnings for damp pink eyes. My nose—slightly reminiscent of my father's, if a lone photograph of him is trustworthy—shone red. (Where was my father? Shouldn't he be knocking on the door? Introducing himself? Explaining what the Hell was going on?) An angry welt choked my neck. I did look thinner, as though the stuffing had been knocked out of me and my skin was struggling to catch up, and everything seemed looser, looser and dissolving, breasts in retreat. I pulled up my dress, placed a hand on my stomach, moved it down a deflated thigh. Dropped the dress and sighed, inspected my arms and veiny, piano-fingered hands. All of the marks were there, everywhere: freckles, bruises, traces of cellulite and the scar on my left arm from the afternoon the Shadowman forced me to try carving a flower with a boxcutter. All were accentuated by the horrible florescent lighting, the hellish trick of retail stores back on Earth, designed to depress you into splurging on the more expensive bathing suit. Well, I thought, that seals it. This ain't Heaven.

Peregrinations, again—God, get me off this fucking treadmill. Gold doorknob in my hand, wild rattling. Bashed my knuckles into the heavy white, polka-dotted it pink with my blood. Moved to the writing desk so I could get a running start, and splatted my pink-sundressed bag o' bones. My heart spazzed, as though trying to pump clots, and I wore a groove between desk and door.

Little pool of body curled on the floor, streaked bloody, joint-wobbly. My breath came in obscene gasps; brutalized, orgasmic rushes. All right God, or Whoever, or the Great Nothing, there you have it: blood, sweat, and tears. Happy now?

INT. VELVET'S PURGATORY (HOPEFULLY) OR HELL (?)—MIRROR—TIMELESS

The Shadowman is in the mirror, playing a tiny violin. He is once again dressed in black cashmere, his dark hair gleaming as though under hot lights.

SHADOWMAN

This is the saddest music in the world. It's enough to make me weep leaden tears. It's enough to make

Beethoven weep leaden tears. In fact, I think Beethoven *did* weep leaden tears! You fucked up.

Notes pour forth from the mirror, melodic quavers hooking themselves into the air, pearlescent nails sunk in flesh.

SHADOWMAN

Repeat after me. I will not go mad. I will not go mad. I will not go mad. I will not go mad. I will not go mad. I will not go mad.

He stops playing the violin and smiles.

SHADOWMAN

Too late.

What the fuck was *he* doing here? He'd forced me to follow his instructions, threatened to burn me alive after pulling out my fingernails if I didn't hang myself just so . . . and I was stupid and naïve enough to have entertained the faint hope that if I did what I was told . . . I would be free of him forever. But if this was in fact Hell, then I guess I'm hooped. My bid to make a final getaway appeared to be a miserable failure. I could be stuck in bed with the Shadowman for all Eternity.

I seeped fluids into the soft carpet while the clock needled the same numbers on the wall above me. Swayed to my knees like a dumb animal nosing the air after sleep. I had a sense that my skin was full of holes (partly true—skinless knuckles, scratches, bruises) and out of those holes hung nerve-tufts, with a spirally weight like Slinkies. Patted myself down briefly to make sure the sensation wasn't based in fact—some weird turn-Velvet-into-sludge torture (although I must say I did an admirable job of that myself—why weren't the walls padded? And why did I suddenly think of the garbage-compacter room in *Star Wars*?)—then crawled to the chair. My breathing was still shaky, and with one hand on the chair I heave-panted into the carpet, which smelled of lavender. This made me gag. Floral scents are inadvisable when one has thrown oneself against a wall. Hunched over, I felt my tonsils twist and a chilly sweat surge from my face and neck. My stomach trampolined. Front flip. Back flip. Side aerial. And bum drop. Everything falls back down into place. I got to my feet holding on to the chair, then lowered myself into it. It was a very Zen-looking little chair, all black lacquer and clean lines, with a white satin cushion covered in black Roman numerals. The writing desk that was now before me was also spare and simple black lacquer, with Chinese characters etched around the border. As a child I was desperate to learn to calligraph their curves and flutes, lettering far more luxurious and profound, I thought, than the boring Roman alphabet. But I never learned and eventually it seemed too difficult a thing, one of the expansive ambitions of childhood to be looked back on with wistful flutters of self-pity when a sizable chunk of your ease and time had somehow disappeared.

Thick, yellow legal pad, purple gel pen. I read once that a lot of famous writers wrote on yellow legal pads and I thought about trying it, but I felt I needed something with an attractive cover. And the incongruity of it. Churning forth art on *legal* paper? Was I missing some profound irony? I liked gel pens, although I used them mostly for drawing flowers on jeans, or giving myself a charm bracelet tattoo around my ankle. (Should I have outgrown such practices? *Should* is a hateful word.) Writing required plain cheap pens, blue or black, Spartan Bics or Papermates. Though purple is my favourite colour.

For some time—the clock still read 8:57—I slumped in the chair, head on the desk. My skull bones throbbed. Miniature individual throbbing skulls sat in each of my knuckles, topped with a messy flower of peeled-back skin and drying blood. The right side of my body ached the worst, shoulder felt dislocated and relocated. Here's a tip: when ragdolling yourself against a wall, remember to switch sides. I listened to the sound of my quivery breathing, face felt webbed tight with salt crystals. I didn't know what to do. What could I do? The door wouldn't open, the wall didn't burst (I did) and no one—perhaps my friend Davie the atheist was right—appeared to hear me, or care. Somewhere in the vicinity of my heart faint bells of panic still rang for troops, but I was too exhausted to answer them with any more bright ideas. A horrible feeling of foolishness crept over me, and the flush of shame, so sure was I in the knowledge that I was the butt of an awful joke. A dupe. An easy mark. A laughingstock. So I sat up, queenly, hauling my spine out of my pelvis, smoothed my hair, licked my lips, squared my shoulders and picked up the purple gel pen. My shame-face deepened to the red of rage, and I uncapped the pen and put it to the yellow legal pad. I wrote these words:

I HATE YOU TOO

3

Flat on my back, pain curlicueing in my right shoulder and arm, and down into my hip. I pulled up my dress and saw black bruises like plague welts. Bubonic bruises. Great. Flopped my head back onto the pillow, pointed and flexed my toes. I didn't feel like moving, but at the same time the instinct of a caged animal was thrumming right beneath the surface of my skin, the same surge of frayed energy that ran through me in the hours, maybe days, before I hung up my belt. I swung my legs off the bed, touched my feet to the ground with a wince as though the soles had been whipped, one hand over the black orchids blooming on my hip. Hobbled to the mirror. Was startled to see that the right side of my mouth was swelling, and my cheekbone was covered with a red patch of puff. Don't ask about the bob.

I turned away and looked at the writing desk and chair. There was something soothing and gorgeous about their shiny simplicity, the gleam of the chair's white satin, black Roman-numeraled cushion. So I sat on it, since I couldn't figure out what else to do. The message I'd written to God or Whoever-Was-Laughing-At-Me stared up in large purple script. I folded the page back and picked up the pen.

Hell, or maybe Purgatory (hopefully)
Somewhere, Nowhere

Still 8:57

Today I killed myself. Well, I don't know what day it was, there's no time in this place—the clock so far is stopped at 8:57. But I killed myself, that much is definite. I always believed in Life After Death, and right now I am sorry to have been proven right. I believed in God, too—well, I was pretty certain—but either I was wrong, or God is more vengeful than I anticipated. I feel lucid in this moment though, more so than I remember feeling in a long time—maybe the bashing-myself-on-the-wall histrionics freed my mind. Funny that technique never worked before I landed myself here. Torture for clarity? Made sense to the saints. But I'm hardly one of them. And the Shadowman's still around—following his instructions was a pointless exercise. I don't know what's expected of me now. Maybe nothing. I can't help thinking though—I'm afraid to think otherwise—that this must be a holding cell, a temporary way station.

I paused and looked up at the barred window with the white view. A new horror squirmed over my skin then, a sudden memory retrieved. Throat very tight, heart meeting stomach. No tears, but the hot hard pressure that precedes them, or lingers when there are no more left. *I'm sorry,* I said. *I'm sorry, I'm sorry, I'm sorry, I'm sorry, I'm sorry, I'm sorry, I'm sorry, I'm sorry.* I picked up my pen and wrote:

I miss my mother.

4

I huddled in the sheets, pulled the eyelet over my head. Tried to squeeze my toes, which had gone cold, warm again. The armholes of my dress were soaked, sweat shivers trembled my shoulders. Queasiness made mashed potatoes in my stomach, and I sat up and tipped my head to the ceiling to perform the necessary ten don't-vomit breaths. A picture of my mother sat fixed in my head like a star. The don't-vomit breaths became gasps and then screams, my body a hooked fish. My hands moved down to my throat, finger-vise sealing off the air, until the stopped-up shriek became a shuddering moan.

> *Time irrelevant*
>
> This place is Hell, I'm fairly convinced of it. And the more I think about it, the more I know I deserve it. Those who create Hell for others deserve not escape, but more suffering, don't they? And how ingenious: not fire and brimstone, but an Eternity with the Self and the Shadowman.

A light knock on the wall punctured the void and I dropped the pen. I sat rooted to the chair, not moving, not breathing. Again: this time three knocks. Not pounding: light, tentative, respectful knocking. If I expected anyone to visit me—I hoped—with directions, instructions, information, a welcome wagon or a red-hot poker, I expected they would use the door. (But why would they? Wake up, Dorothy, you're not in Kansas anymore.) Hands on desk, I pushed myself from the chair, knees buckling once. The knocking had come from the wall just above the bed. I made it to the middle of the room before I stopped, arms crossed snug over my chest. Listened. Nothing but silence. I weighed my options, and faced with an Eternity of cudgelling loneliness, moved forward and climbed onto the bed. Clinging to one of the white bedposts, I waited some more, listening to my heart pump out warning. The air was dense, murky and hot. No more knocks. I leaned in and placed my fingertips on the wall, then leaned in further, grinding my ear into the pink. An auditory mirage? I drew back and curled my fingers into a fist and poised it, as if ready to fire. Knocked with the side of my hand, two, three. Then darted my fist into my other hand, ball into glove, eyes wide and burning. *One Mississippi, two Mississippi, three Mississippi*—I gripped the headboard—*four Mississippi*—fingers whitening—*five Mississippi*—cramp in my neck—*six Mississ—knock, knock, knock.* I unfroze, pulling my hands into my chest. The knocking was hard, a pepper of sound. My breathing sped to short chugs and I answered one two, three four, five six. Response: one two three, four five six, seven, eight—pause—nine. I pounded back a rhythm, then painted the wall with my hands looking for some unseen opening, a soft spot, a *Star Trek* portal. But in no place did my fingers melt through. The skin around my eyes stung from salt. The room was clamped in a silence that produced its own sound, a sucking—an aural leech. I banged out another pattern. And another. There was no answer. No pattern, no rhythm now: my hands covered the wall in a volley of slap-knocking. Nothing, nothing—nothing. I pulled my stinging, mashed-up hands away, puddled onto the eyelet.

Someone had knocked on my wall—I heard it. Or was I being driven crazy(er)? I stared at the ceiling. The bee-buzzing lightness of a fever-dream.

Possible escape routes, magic loopholes, chinks in the cosmic armour: nada, zip, dream on, outta luck, no way. I moved the bed, moved the desk, moved the mirror, pummelled the walls of the closet, whimpered at the door like a discarded puppy, attempted—without success—to rip up the carpet and briefly considered trying to hang myself from the doorknob.

(Karmic double indemnity? Kill yourself twice—ride the soul train to Heaven? Oh, the sweet wishes of Hell. . . .) I did discover, to my temporary ecstasy, a small metallic grate, like an air vent, on the wall near the floor, in the corner into which the bed was wedged, and made more bloody work of my hands trying to pry it free and reveal what I was convinced was going to be a highway to Heaven. Okay, so it wouldn't budge. Plan B: shout into it, try to make alien contact. My screams must have deafened the Devil.

HELLLLPPPPP! HELLLLLLPPPP! ANYONE THERE? ANYONE HOME? ARE YOU FUCKING DEAF?

(Well, now they are, whoever *they* is.)

After wearing out my voice, attempting to dam my tears and snot, pulling out my eyelashes and then finally replacing all the furnishings—somehow it seemed necessary to keep the Pit of Doom neat and tidy—my nerves kept me pacing, as though if I walked fast enough, spun around in the blink of an eye, I could jump clear of my skin. Back and forth, wearing a fashion model groove in the carpet. Each time I turned from the closet, I startled at the fresh snapshot of myself in the mirror, botched-up fat-lipped cover girl. Out of my face's collage of colours, my black eyes glittered like lonely coal pits. The wall was quiet. I used the hem of my dress to dab at the sweat under my arms. My neck felt giraffe-like, tall and swaying. The room alternated between stasis and sudden tilting, and I leaned against the slant, sometimes grasping a bedpost, trying to stay on my feet, to keep marching through the tipping ether.

A giant lurch and over she goes—I lay on my side breathing the faint lavender scent of the carpet, feeling my ribs tighten their cat's cradle. I beamed wide unseeing eyes into the dimness beneath the dust-ruffled bed (I wanted a bed like this? Nothing is more embarrassing than the person you used to be) and rocked forward and back, forward and back. The room's silence hummed like a minting factory for new souls.

And then I saw something.

White beyond the white of the dust ruffle, like a hand coming out of the twilight. I squeezed my eyes shut and opened them. The flash of white remained, so I wiggled half-under the ruffle and stretched out my arm. I poked at the white with my index finger, prepared for heat or corrosive material.

It was a piece of paper.

I closed my hand around the cool crinkle and rolled out into the full light of the room. White legal paper, folded ever so neatly with sharp creases like a starched and ironed shirt. I chewed my peeling lips. I opened the paper.

To Whom It May Concern:

I heard you knocking and I was very excited. I am alone in this room. I would really like to know the answers to two questions. They are:

Who are you?

Why are you there?

Please write back. If you cannot, please knock three times. If you need paper, knock four times, and I will send you a piece. I do not think I can fit a pen through the grate, and anyway, I only have one.

Yours very truly,

Brinkley

I read the note three times. And then I read it three more. I read it until the letters started to float off the page and gymnastic into other letters. *Brinkley.* I sat propped up by the bed, one hand clinging to the ruffle, the other to the note. The room's stillness framed my own. My lips tingled.

I was not alone.

I thought back to when I was first dumped at this Motel-6-in-the-Ether, (was God a plebeian? Certainly a philistine) to all of the identical tall, white doors with their identical large gold knobs. Was it possible that behind each and every one of them was another hapless sad sack without a clue? This was decidedly not a letter from God, or the Devil, or anyone who knew what was going on. *Brinkley.* I said the name several times aloud. I liked it. I turned the paper over again and again, even though I knew that the back was blank, just to make sure that there wasn't any spontaneously appearing map and instructions on how to get the Hell out of here. (My own brand of optimism refused to die in full, and that, I concluded, was one of the Torturer's screws. Hope is a cruel thing.)

"To Whom It May Concern." To Whom It May Concern? Who opens a letter from Hell with that header? I studied the handwriting, made up my mind that Brinkley was a boy. Or rather, a man. The letters were plain, even blocky, though precise and neat.

"Who are you?" Well there's a question for the ages.

Dear Brinkley,

I decked myself out and hung myself up. Too bad I ended up here, but good thing I was wearing a nice outfit and all my bills were paid on time. . . .

No thanks. Though come to think of it, what did I care? The worst had happened, and what's the point of trying to uphold your reputation in Hell? I turned my yellow legal pad to a fresh page, picked up my pen, and scrawled:

Dear Brinkley,

Receiving your letter was definite cause for celebration. I too am alone in my room. My name is Velvet. I lived in Vancouver, Canada. I committed suicide, and then I came here. I don't know how long I've been here, maybe five minutes, maybe forever. The clock on my wall is stopped at 8:57—anyway, time seems irrelevant. This is definitely not Heaven, and until I got your letter I was convinced it's Hell. Now I'm not so sure. I flirted with the idea of Purgatory, some kind of rest stop, but I certainly have not been restful and there is a decided lack of further instructions, hoops of fire to jump through, skill-testing questions to answer, etc. If you have any insights into this predicament, I would be grateful.

Now I ask the same two questions of you: who are you and why are you there?

Sincerely, Velvet

I pushed my letter through the grate and waited in the shade under the bed, lying on my side with my arms and legs drawn into me, as though in a carpeted womb. The bright lights of the rest of the room seemed sinister, marauding. And I was afraid that being exposed to them would somehow cause me to miss what I hoped was Brinkley's forthcoming letter.

There was no dust under the bed. The lavender smell had an antiseptic edge. This womb was sterile.

I closed my eyes and listened for the rustle of paper. I had Brinkley's letter clutched in my left hand, a reassurance that I hadn't hallucinated a correspondence. Every few moments I would press it to my face, as though my hand was no longer feeling it, and I had to remind myself that it was there. I touched my tongue to it, too, and it tasted like real paper.

Venus flytrap, my hand snapped at the letter as it came through the grate. In my excitement, I rolled over, sat up and brained myself on the bed. Clutching my head, I poked it from the womb, into the bright lights of Hell, and started to read.

Dear Velvet,

I was likewise overjoyed to receive your letter. Velvet is a pretty name. Were you named after someone, or were your parents trying to be original? My mother was a painter, and I suffered for her love of originality. When I was growing up, the kids at school called me Wrinkly.

I am very sorry to learn of the circumstances that brought you here. I am not as clear on why I find myself in this room. Truth be told, the last thing I remember is running along a street on my way to work. I was starting a new job, and I was afraid I was going to be late. I darted off a curb headed for my usual café and my soy latte (I am allergic to cow's milk) when suddenly I found myself whizzing down a slide in the dark, and eventually wound up here. Having had considerable opportunity to reflect, I have decided that in all likelihood a car ran me over. I remember that two nights before my ill-fated excursion, I had a dream that I was hit by a speeding yellow Volkswagen Beetle on my way to work. I woke up sweaty, like I had been running a marathon in my sleep (I am not a very athletic person), and with the definite feeling that I should not leave the house. I still felt that way the following morning and I thought about calling in sick, but it was the first day of my new job, and so I really was not able to, and I pushed whatever misgivings I had out of my mind. Gee whiz, whoever said, "always trust your instincts" was not kidding. I have learned that the hard way.

Who am I? That is a difficult question to answer, is it not? I lived in Toronto. I worked at a bank. I guess you could say I am a numbers guy.

I apologize for the fact that I can provide no more answers than you. I, too, have no idea how long I have been here—the clock on my wall is stopped at 8:56. I was growing sure that this indeed is Hell—or a Hell of sorts, there's no denying that—and I have been wracking my brain trying to figure out what I did to deserve this. I suppose there might be a few things.

But now that I know you are there, so close, I do not know what to think. Please tell me your thoughts.

Yours very truly,
Brinkley

So my neighbour, apparently, was just as clueless as I was. (Tell him my thoughts? *Help me! Somebody help me!*) I lay under the bed, head poked into the light, tracing his handwriting with my eyes. The pieces of the jigsaw that I thought I had pushed together promptly broke apart. If he was telling the truth, and why hold back, he wasn't a suicide, and he hadn't murdered anyone with a blunt instrument. He was the victim of a harried morning commuter. So why was he trapped next to me? The hair-on-fire evangelist that I had watched on TV once at age nine said that even small, unrepented sins would land you in the Pit. Remembering this, Mandarin-nailed fingers started to drum in my chest. I refused to believe he was right.

The light in the room (where was it coming from? There weren't any lamps) glared like sun off glass, and my eyes ached. I retracted my head into the dusky under-bed cave, called up my head's Greek senate to debate what to write next. I didn't want to keep Brinkley waiting long—I knew well the horror of being on hold. My mind was chattering its loquacious best. The sweetish lavender scent of the carpet strengthened, an olfactory knockout punch. My feet were numb, and the weighty deadness of my legs frightened me. I lifted my calves, shook them and let them drop, then kicked furiously to dash paralysis fears. To the desk, but first: the mirror. It had the look of a liquid transparency, so clean and clear was the glass. Staring at it, I almost expected it to ripple, or splash like dropped mercury. My haunted face in the water of it recalled Plath's fear of the terrible fish. Wrinkled, bloodstained dress, hollowed-out collarbone, bruised face and hedgeclippered hair. But my eyes, always black-coffee, had begun to glow blue around the edge of the iris. Electric, wild stare. Microwaved. I stood, blinking slowly, wondering if the passing over of my eyelid would erase the line. It stayed fixed: hard lapis.

INT. VELVET'S HELL—MIRROR—VELVET'S BATHROOM—TIMELESS

The Shadowman is now styled as Zorro, his black cape blowing out behind him as though he is standing in front of a giant fan. In one hand he clutches the belt that Velvet used to hang herself, and attached to the belt is Velvet herself, neck bent like a broken bird's, limp and lifeless. He shakes her, hoists her high like dead quarry.

SHADOWMAN

Say hi little girl. Who's your daddy?

At the desk I sat trembling and trying to pull out my eyelashes, though I had already done a thorough job of that. I poked at my morphing eyes. Their changing colours, the doom marks on my irises, had not altered my vision at all. My Hell still looked the same.

Dear Brinkley,

I must say I was thrown by your description of the circumstances that landed you here. Because of my own story, I was convinced that this was a place for suicides and axe murderers, and those who have otherwise botched their karma. But you were an innocent victim; in fact, you can't even quite remember what happened to you. So that detonates my theory and I'm—if it's possible—even more confused. You said that there were things you might have done to deserve this. Such as?

Like you, I was sure that this is Hell, but now that I know you're next door, and we're able to communicate, I'm wavering. Have we found a cosmic loophole? Is this really what it's like to be dead? Perhaps there's no use mowing this grass anymore, since neither of us has any idea and until something comes along to rattle our cages, we will remain among the clueless.

So you're a banker. I relied on my Snoopy calculator for everything. I was one of the kids that took dummy math in high school—I knew the mathematics of putting together a great outfit though, which frankly helps when your teacher's a lech and you're trying to pass the course. I worked as a waitress at a Thai café on Commercial Drive—I lived just off of there. You'd think I would've picked up a few tricks of the trade, absorbed some culinary skill through osmosis, but instead I was just the café's best customer. I really can't cook at all. I once cooked spaghetti for my friend Davie and he had heartburn for three days, and even my Bisquick pancakes turned green. Eating was by far my most successful relationship to food.

As for my name, my mother called me Velvet. The first time she felt me kick she was hanging velvet drapes. And yes, I suffered for it. The kids at school called me Velveeta.

Maybe we're now film stars playing out some warped chucklefest on the Devil's movie screen. We still haven't seen the Devil, which makes everything more terrifying. I'd take a pitchfork over nebulous evil any day. The Devil must find Kafka hysterically funny.

I wonder if there's anyone else trapped in adjacent rooms. I keep thinking of the actor George Sanders, whose suicide note read:

"Dear World, I am leaving because I am bored."
We could be in the presence of a celebrity.
Sincerely, Velvet
P.S. My eyes appear to be turning from blackish to blue. Are you experiencing any changes in your appearance?

The pocket of dim under the bed started to suffocate, the smell of lavender beginning to take on aerosol room spray intensity. I poked my head out from under the dust ruffle. The closet door still stood wide open, the lone hanger's single talon gripping its perch. The sight of the empty shelves and naked bars made me think of moving day. Bereft closets have always made me feel sad. I pulled my head back to the darker side of the dust ruffle, holding my breath, and felt around the grate for a letter. My fingers moved over it compulsively, up and down, even though I knew that Brinkley wouldn't have finished his letter yet. Or so I guessed. Without Time, it was impossible to calculate. In a Black Hole, *when?* is not a relevant question. I cupped the sides of my face and brought an eye to the grate, feeling my lashes swish against metal. The bars were fitted tightly together and I strained to see through the slivers of space between them. My eye bulged with effort, searching for a glimmer of light, a moving shadow. But everything was black. Pain fireworked behind my eyes, from staring at nothing.

Rushed my head out into the light. For a moment the room was tulle-ed in a vertiginous blur. I shook my head and slithered the rest of me out from under.

I crawled to the closet. It was deep and large, made all the more so by its emptiness. The hanger twisted right and then left, over and over, almost imperceptibly, as though creating a rhythm to make up for the motionless clock. I crawled inside, ran the blade of one hand up and down the right angle of a corner. Turned and sat, hanger an overhead beacon. I thought of my red dress.

The gilt angels 'round the mirror stared at me with looks of dumb love and unhelpful innocence. Purity can be a real bitch.

INT. VELVET'S HELL—MIRROR—VELVET'S BATHROOM—TIMELESS

The woman with the psychotic bob hangs in her bathroom, fashionable Death channelling itself through a vintage lizard skin belt. Life drains in a series of colours in her face, nearing the exit with an ashy pale. She sways, graceful and grotesque. The Shadowman enters, wearing a tuxedo. He grasps the hanging woman around her waist and clasps one of her hands.

SHADOWMAN

(smiling)

Velvet, my darling girl.

He begins to ballroom dance with her on the spot, singing "I Could Have Danced All Night" from *My Fair Lady*.

The sound of the glass shattering, and the blood on my hands: these were the things that my senses remembered, not the intricacies of each moment's memory. Screams pealed at the walls: they must have been my own, unless the Devil has my voice. On my knees on the carpet, bloody hands and burning tears, and a buzzing fog that obscured the far-off flashing lights. I touched the blood to my lips, tasted the metal. My insides were easily swallowed, their taste evoking some forgotten hunger.

Face to the carpet and fingers in ears, my dress twisted and bunched 'round my torso. When my eyes opened, they remained naïve for several moments to the rough expanse before them. The room swelled and shifted like a mirage in the desert sun as I sat up, haloed with glitter. My dress was splotched with wrung bloodstains, a horror movie tie-dyed affair. The dyeing instruments, though, were much restored: the cuts on my hands had healed to mere hairline fractures. I wiped my mouth and took a big, slow breath, trying to fashion the unreality of the room and the unreality of my memories into a wearable idea, a plausible truth, if not a pound of real flesh, then a paper doll. There was no glass on the carpet. The mirror hung whole and perfect on the wall.

INT. VELVET'S HELL—MIRROR—TIMELESS

The man in the mirror is slight, with sloping shoulders. His eyes are green, encircled in blue. He stands very still, a look of struck wonder captive on his features. A soft, small, tentative smile urges his lips. He raises a hand, his motion halting yet smooth, as though moving undersea. The hand reaches out, palm flat, seeking touch.

I reached out my hand, resting the palm against the man's in the glass. His eyes were liquid with wonder. He was a stranger to me, and yet as familiar as my own shadow.

Dear Velvet,

Was it you I saw? Did you see me? A beautiful woman appeared in my mirror and placed her palm to mine. You? Very black eyes (bluish borders) and brown, sort of curly hair, cut kind of like Clara Bow's, if you know who I mean. She looked so familiar to me, even though I didn't recognize her, like someone I knew so long ago that I remember only the feeling of knowing them, not the actual person. And then she disappeared and I was left with my own reflection, which I hate. I cried to see it, and not the woman, standing before me. She must be you, Velvet. I am sure of it. Please come back to me.

My own reflection—perhaps you saw it?—is as disappointing as ever. I still cannot lay claim to a chin, or a smaller nose. But since this is clearly not Heaven, what can I expect? I suppose I should be grateful that I do not have plague welts sprouting from my cheeks. (I just knocked on wood, though the protective effects of that are doubtful.) My eyes, like yours, are turning blue and, like you, I cannot begin to guess why. It is a very strange thing to be terrified by the sight of your own eyes. But then again, when I think about it, I realize that this feeling is nothing new.

My hands are killing me—no pun intended. I pushed back two of my knuckles trying to pound my way out of here. I have never punched anything before. Once I started, I could not stop. It was like some manner of frenzy possessed me, the way animals become possessed without care or reason. My right hand split open and I got blood on my white shirtfront, and some on my suit jacket, but it is black—the jacket, not the blood—so it is not visible. Not that it matters. But I really hate blood, and I have this thing about being clean—I always washed my shirts twice in scalding hot water (and my dresses, but that is a different story)—so I have taken off the jacket and shirt and put them in the closet. Although I suppose scientifically speaking blood is not unhygienic, but it might be once it makes contact with wool and cotton—forgive me, I digress. I closed the closet door, but I know the bloody stuff is in there and it is really driving me crazy. I have always been a pacer when I get upset, but in here—well, what else is there to do? I get so frantic at times that I throw open the closet door, thinking there is something for me to organize, and then I am confronted with the pierce of space between the empty shelves, and the blot of bloody jacket and shirt. I have been remaking the bed, trying to get the bulges out, but the lumps keep coming back. The sheets have red and blue and yellow cars all over them, like the kind I had when I was a child. A painful sight. I still like them.

Will you describe your neighbourhood to me, please? How long had you worked at that café? Did you live alone?

Yours very truly,
Brinkley

His dresses? Was he a drag queen? Somehow, I doubted it. So did he play dress-up alone in his room? Well, I can hardly fault anyone for that. Maybe I'm next door to a nouveau version of Ed Wood.

I sat in front of the Chinese screen cross-legged, tracing the green flicks of bamboo leaves with my finger. There were characters on the right side, which I imagined comprised a poem, or instructions on how to escape. At the bottom, two small birds, nearly invisible in shades of green and brown, their beaks delicate needlepoints, gazed at one another as if across a bamboo-filled chasm.

My mother had kept a similar screen in the living room, with the same bends of foliage and tea tones tinged with gold, except there were three birds instead of two. She said it was the only gift that my father ever bought her.

I ran my finger over the characters, as though I might decipher their meaning by touch. The single eye on each of the birds shone satiny black. I wished for some sort of post-mortem mail delivery system, a vent through which I could push a letter to my mother. The flats of my hands came to rest on the cool parchment, as I imagined them against her face.

Dear Brinkley,

I saw you too! It must have been you. Green eyes (bluish borders), brown, very neatly parted hair. (How does your hair stay so neat when you're trying to punch your way out of the room? Obviously, you have hair tips that I'm missing.) You looked so familiar to me as well, familiar and strange at once, like the picture of a longing for some fragile figment of memory.

Before you appeared to me, I smashed the mirror. At least I think I did, though the only evidence of that now is the bloodstain on my dress. The mirror is once again whole and perfect on the wall (obviously, or I wouldn't have seen you), and the gashes on my hands are healed, with only faint lines where I remember gushing wounds. I can't trust my memory—could we trust it before? It's like I'm trapped in my own mind. There's nothing more horrible than being left to the vagaries of one's head—what a capricious enemy! And even if you tell the enemy to fuck off, even if you know her as you know yourself, you can never kill her. The mind shifts like the tides. What a splendid Hell.

Right at present the mirror shows me nothing but a faithful reflection of my room, and myself, a reflection tuned, as always, to the frequency governed by a prevailing sense of self-hatred, despair and now-justified phobias. You're the only one able to see my new, shockingly stick-figured self. (Finally I'm in fashion but the audience has grown so scant.) Back in life, I always had a figure that I categorized like clothing: vintage. I kept pictures of women from the '30s, '40s and '50s all over my walls, to remind myself that the fleshy hourglass is beautiful. Stuck on my fridge with a *Sunset Boulevard* fridge magnet were the words: "Today's Miss America contestant is 23% thinner than contestants in the 1960s." Not that I care at all about the Miss America pageant, but it helped me keep modern society's rot in perspective. However, looking in the mirror now I can say that I look even thinner than today's pageant girls.

I can see my ribs, several Mona Lisa smiles, which were certainly things I once had to conduct a concentrated search for.

I want to see you again. I didn't think it was me at first that you saw . . . you described the woman as beautiful. But then you mentioned the Clara Bow hair. Actually, I was thinking of Louise Brooks when I cut it. Or maybe I wasn't really thinking . . . I was following instructions. What can you do with hair that resembles offshore storms on the Weather Channel, or with a face like an inverted egg, eyes shadowy as an absinthe addict's? Though I was never an absinthe addict. I decided it must be me that you saw, unless there's some poor loony on the other side of you who spent her final moments attempting to channel a silent film star through a pair of dull scissors.

Here's some more info, if you like: I lived alone in a lower floor suite of a "heritage house," which is really just a polite term for an old place in need of repairs. The street I lived on was lined with trees, including a very large one in my front yard. I loved to watch the sky pool in the branches in the early morning. For as long as I can remember, I dreamed about living on a tree-lined street. So the sidewalk forest was the thing that spurred me into renting the place (that and the fact that I had no money), when my senses were assaulted by the rather crumbling suite with its splintery hardwood floors. The house itself was 1920s clapboard with frilly latticework. It was purple, with unfortunate hot pink trim. Purple is my favourite colour, but it belongs in a closet, not on a house.

Commercial Drive is a bohemian street, although it falls way short of Montparnasse-circa-1910's definition of bohemian. It's full of artists and good restaurants and men with dreadlocked hair and women carrying loom-spun purses. It used to be Little Italy—all in all, it's kind of like "Socialism Meets Gelato."

I had worked at the Thai café for a year, long enough to become addicted to coconut milk. Before that, I did some time in the coat check of a bar, which, aside from allowing me the opportunity to test out some inventive outfits, was a nightmarish cave of sweaty-fleshed, sex-hungry mongrels. I prefer to stay away from that sort of thing. I was planning to quit, but before I had the chance I had a panic attack and broke a bottle of Glenlivet, and was told in a not-very-nice-way never to return. So my friend Davie came over to talk me down from the eaves, so to speak, because I was slightly hysterical about being jobless and behind in my rent. But, as usual, he smoothed everything out. He called his friend Mrs. Wong, who owns a photocopy place, and told her to call up her brother and tell him that she had found the perfect waitress for his new café. So that's how I got the job. Davie saved the day again. Then he wanted to talk about his relationship problems—as per usual. And yes, the owners, Harry and Carrie, are Chinese, but they felt that the Vancouver market was a little saturated with Chinese restaurants.

I miss Davie so much.

Brinkley—who have you left behind? I didn't have many friends, except for Davie. I had a mother. I miss them so much sometimes I can't breathe and I wonder what would happen if I stopped breathing in this place. I did a bad thing. Do you think they hate me? I was only doing the inevitable—I had been hunted for so long.

How can we stay here, Brinkley, with the weight of missing those we will never see pressing us between invisible stones?

Sincerely, Velvet

P.S. I understand the desperation of wanting to organize the closet. I feel the same way—although I was never an exceptionally organized person in general, just a lady who was very particular about how her couture collection was arranged. All right—now that I've reached the P.S. part of the letter, I'll come right out and ask, since you must want me to, or you wouldn't have brought it up—you wash your *dresses* in scalding water? Or did you mean your mother's dresses? It seemed like you were talking about your own clothes. Were you a drag queen? Or like the film director Ed Wood? His wife said that he derived maternal comfort from angora in particular. I get that. Or did you own some sort of doll collection?

P.P.S. My sheets here have rainbows and clouds on them, just like when I was a little girl. I still like them, too.

I cuddled myself between my rainbow and cloud sheets. True: I did still like them, but in a different place, a place with working clocks and people. (Why did I long for people? I was never great at communicating with them in life, and the man that haunted my lonely hours was not exactly a fuzzy friend and chucklefest travelling companion. And, naturally, I suppose, he was still coming around to make my life—or non-life—a living Hell.) But here, the bright pink pinkness of them, the insistent cheer, together with the smiling glassy-eyed faces of plush toys, was sinister, a menagerie of longing. I stared hard at the ceiling so I wouldn't have to look at the Chinese screen and think of my mother, and started to count the little plaster bumps, my old habit. *One, two, three, four, five*—no, wait—*one, two, three, four, five, six*—no—*one, two*—The old splintery club of pain thwacked behind my eyes, bludgeoning my focus. My fingers clutched at my bellybutton, trying to push the panic down toward spastic toes. *One, two, three*—all the dots melt together, red food colouring overtaking a glass of clear water. The counted and the uncounted mix together; there is no way to know which ones I must get to. Hands a flesh-clamp over the eyes, to keep back the tide of bumps.

5

Swish, swish, went my lashes against cloth—eyes comparing the dark beneath my lids to the dark of the eyeshade. I had found it, the eyeshade, in a tiny drawer hidden on the right side of my writing desk. Hot pink satin, fringed in feathers and brought to life by cartoon eyes, it fit snugly and blocked the ceiling bumps from view. So there was some grace in this place.

I was curled on my side, the only position in which I could ever lie comfortably on a bed, despite many attempts at reforming myself into a back-sleeper to prevent early-onset crow's feet. I listened to the silence. Not the quiet, or the polyglot strains of white noise from the relaxation tapes I once tried, but the true, utter, ten-thousand-leagues-below silence of my pink room. I lay in the dry heart of the sea.

I imagined the footfalls of my mother approaching the door, the clink of ice in her glass. I imagined myself standing outside my childhood bedroom door in clown pajamas (Given Paddington Bear and his band of merry stuffed animals, I'm surprised I wasn't provided with a set, complete with a matching security blanket.) waiting for her to come back from a date, green shag carpeting sprouting through my toes.

6

INT. BRINKLEY'S HELL—MIRROR—
VELVET'S CHILDHOOD HOME—BACKYARD—AFTERNOON

Velvet is a young girl. She sits cross-legged in the grass. The sun ripples everything with fever. Velvet holds a pencil and a notebook. On it she writes Roman numerals. Velvet's mother comes stumbling out of the house, drunk, wearing a full, crimson Spanish skirt and armfuls of heavy, jangling gold bangles.

MOTHER

(slurring)
Whatcha doin'?

VELVET

I'm counting sounds. Bird sounds.

MOTHER

How many?

VELVET

Fifteen.

MOTHER

Noisy fuckers.

VELVET

They like to sing.

MOTHER

(singing at the top of her lungs)

"It's my party, and I'll cry if I want to
Cry if I want to . . ."

VELVET

Ssshhh! You'll scare them off!

MOTHER

Fine. Party pooper.

All is quiet for a moment. Velvet stares into space, pen poised to record another birdcall. Her mother picks at a loose thread on the hem of her skirt. Then: pounce! Like a cat on yarn, Velvet's mother is on her, pulling at her hair and smothering her with kisses.

VELVET

(shoving her)

Get off me!

Her mother yanks a handful of grass and throws it at her daughter, pouting.

MOTHER

You're just like your father.

Velvet holds out her arms.

VELVET

I'm sorry, Mom, I'm sorry. Cuddle me.

MOTHER

No. I don't want to anymore.

INT. BRINKLEY'S HELL—MIRROR—
VELVET'S CHILDHOOD HOME—KITCHEN—EVENING

Velvet's mother stands at the stove, stir-frying meat and vegetables. An open bottle of gin sits on the counter, and every once in a while she takes a swig and then pours some into her wok. She wears a tight, sky-blue dress cut from a T-shirt type material, a get-up that announces her lack of undergarments to the world, and ultra-high heels.

On the kitchen floor sits Velvet, a bottle of crimson nail polish in hand, and she waves the brush through the air as though painting it: Sally Hansen-cum-Picasso. Her feet are ornamented with nail polish flowers, each with distinctive impeccable petals: chemical-scented, hothouse blooms. She begins to bestow an ankle with like adornment.

MOTHER

What the hell are you doing to yourself?

VELVET

Nail polish tattoos.

MOTHER

(laughs)

What's possessed you?

VELVET

That home and garden show. They showed those flower decals that you put in the shower so you don't slip and kill yourself.

MOTHER

Oh. Well, you've got the flowers on the wrong side of your feet if you're worried about slipping and killing yourself.

VELVET

What time's he coming?

MOTHER

Twenty minutes. Put some socks on.

VELVET

I can't. Polish's still wet. And what's the point of decorating your feet if you're going to wear socks?

MOTHER

Oh for fuck's sake.

(pause)

How do I look? Look at my new shoes. I blew the bank. Italian leather. Like buttah!

VELVET

You want my honest opinion?

MOTHER

No. Yes. Not really.

VELVET

(sizing her up)

You look good. You always look good. The picture of sweetness and light.

MOTHER

Oh you're an angel! Why don't you make yourself a tinfoil halo? Sweetness and light! Ha ha! Lie to me some more.

(pause)

So, you really think I look all right?

VELVET

You look like Mae West. Well, your face does, anyway. Maybe you should dye your hair blonde.

MOTHER

I've thought about it. Hmmm . . . shit, I should've made a drugstore run for Clairol. Ha! Mae West, you say. Well, I do all my best work in bed.

She takes a long drink from the gin bottle.

MOTHER

Shit, I'm nervous. I'm a nervous wreck. I'm a wrecked bundle of nerves. Okay. You remember what I told you?

VELVET

When the doorbell rings, take the fruit rollups and stay upstairs.

MOTHER

Good girl.

(pause)

Do I look fat?

INT. BRINKLEY'S HELL—MIRROR—
VELVET'S CHILDHOOD HOME—BEDROOM—NIGHT

Velvet sits on the floor of her bedroom, with three red fruit rollups draped across her lap. She points and flexes her nail polish-flowered feet.

VELVET

Rather fetching, don't you think, Delilah?

Her mother's raucous laughter, together with a deep male voice, drifts up the stairs to Velvet's ears.

INT. BRINKLEY'S HELL—MIRROR—
VELVET'S CHILDHOOD HOME—KITCHEN—CONTINUOUS

A short white candle cries waxy tears down an empty wine bottle on the kitchen table. The sky-blue blueness of Velvet's mother's T-shirt dress looks icy in the candlelight as it melts over an epicure's wobbling flesh. The woman herself is seated at the table, smoke from her cigarette curling upward like a prayer. The man with olive skin also smokes, the pungent stream from his cigar rising alongside her offering in a competition for benediction. Both drink whisky.

The Mae West look-alike (sans platinum locks), scrapes her fingers on the bottom of her empty chocolate mousse bowl, without looking at it, as though she's trying to read some sort of culinary Braille. Every once in a while she sticks them in her mouth and sucks, relishing the scant vestiges of dessert.

Olive Man is telling a story and Mae/Mother laughs all through it, choking on her drink and spitting some back in her glass.

OLIVE MAN

You all right, honey?

Mae West nods, still choking. Olive Man pours the last of the whisky into his tumbler and downs it in a swallow. She stumbles out of her chair and onto his lap, straddling him. She grabs one of his hair-covered hands and places it on her breast.

MAE/MOTHER

(coughing)

Wanna go upstairs? My daughter's asleep.

OLIVE MAN

You have a daughter?

INT. BRINKLEY'S HELL—MIRROR—VELVET'S CHILDHOOD HOME—BEDROOM—CONTINUOUS

Velvet rips her red fruit rollups into little strips and begins braiding them. The sounds of Mae/Mother's choking laughter and Olive Man's baritonic slurs surge in a cacophonous tide up the stairs. The fruit leather tapestry needs no attention—the stylist is adept—and so Velvet focuses her gaze on the black outside her window, on the moon hung like a congealed and sculpted tear.

VELVET

(sings softly)

"Two drifters, off to see the world
There's such a lot of world to see . . ."

MAE/MOTHER

(O.S.)

I get these fucking headaches. Night after night.

There is a loud thump.

MAE/MOTHER

(O.S) (laughing)

Get off! Wait 'til we get upstairs. Ssshhh! You'll wake up my daughter!

Velvet stuffs all her fruit rollup braids in her mouth, but doesn't chew them. She crawls to her door, which is ajar, and peers into the hallway.

INT. BRINKLEY'S HELL—MIRROR—VELVET'S CHILDHOOD HOME—UPSTAIRS HALLWAY—CONTINUOUS

Mae/Mother crawls up the last couple of stairs with Olive Man on top of her, pulling off her dress.

MAE/MOTHER

(loudly)

Holy fuck! I think I'm . . . a little tipsy!

She is naked, and Olive Man's shirt hangs open. He is pulling off his belt.

MAE/MOTHER

Ssshhh! Be quiet!

Olive Man dives on top of her, wraps his belt around her neck.

MAE/MOTHER

Ow! Watch it! Oh yeah . . .

(laughs)

"A hard man is good to find!" I'm quoting! That's a quote!

Velvet watches, half hidden by her door. Fruit rollup braids sprout from her mouth.

Mae/Mother pulls off the belt.

MAE/MOTHER

Wait! Inside, inside! No!

(laughs)

Bed, I said bed! Ssshhh! Quiet!

A cuckoo clock on the wall explodes in a frenzy of squawking, sounding the discordant hour.

MAE/MOTHER

Shit! I hate that fucking clock!

Olive Man devours her mouth. His pants have come down around his knees. The watchbird on the wall continues to crow.

MAE/MOTHER

(between kisses)

Shut . . . the . . . fuck . . . up . . . you . . . stupid . . . bird! Oh!

Olive Man's underwear goes south. His buttocks are white and gleaming as the moon—the goddess Diana is appalled. He enters Mae/Mother; their two bodies loll and thrash on the carpet. A cry escapes from her throat, while guttural groans exit from his. Velvet, in her doorway, plugs her ears and closes her eyes, chews her fruit rollup braids. In a moment she opens her eyes, unplugs her ears and wraps her arms around herself. Olive Man again wraps his belt around Mae/Mother's throat. A broken crying rhythmic chant replaces the din of the clock. As banshees from bellies, screeches pour forth. The shrieking woman clings to the belt, yanking it loose, while the shrieking man holds fast to fistfuls of his lady's hair. Velvet covers her mouth with her hands. A final howl, a dual petition to the moon, bays through the ceiling. Gasping and glistening, Mae/Mother and Olive Man lie supine on the floor.

MAE/MOTHER

Oh . . .
(laughs)
Baby . . .

OLIVE MAN

Huh?

MAE/MOTHER

I said bed . . .

Velvet closes her door.

INT. BRINKLEY'S HELL—MIRROR—
VELVET'S CHILDHOOD HOME—VELVET'S BEDROOM—LATER

Out the window and into the night—Velvet kneels on her bed with her face pressed to the glass. The moon is violent in its brightness. A wind has its way with the trees. Velvet blows on the window and writes Roman numerals in the fog, her finger squeaking against the glass. She pauses in her artistry, and the quietness is full and unbroken, a Zen circle. A punch to an unseeing eye—brawling yells from the room next door, a motley chorus of pitches and tones, assault the silent circle. Velvet freezes, then melts into motion toward her door. She opens it, slow and tentative.

INT. BRINKLEY'S HELL—MIRROR—
VELVET'S CHILDHOOD HOME—HALLWAY—CONTINUOUS

Mae/Mother's bedroom door is partly ajar, but not open enough to reveal the room's contents. Velvet sits crouched in her doorway.

MAE/MOTHER

(O.S.)

You fucking prick! Fuck!

There is a crash.

MAE/MOTHER

Off!

She begins to scream.

MAE/MOTHER

Get away from me!

OLIVE MAN

You fucking bitch! You fucking cu—Ow!!!

There is another crash. More screams. Velvet is crying.

VELVET

(screaming)

Mom! Mom! Mom!

Olive Man stampedes from the bedroom in his underwear, an unpenned bull. His clothes a rolled-up ball under one arm. He dervishes down the stairs, stumbling and falling into the railing. Mae/Mother staggers from her bedroom, bleeding from her nose and mouth. She stands at the top of the stairs.

MAE/MOTHER

AAAAAAAAAHHHHHHHHHHHHHH!!!!!!!!!!!!

Olive Man yanks open the front door and charges at the night. Mae/Mother crumples like a bloody tissue, her forehead pressed to the stair railing, and wails. Then she is silent. The only noise is that of a car starting up and roaring away. Velvet, still crying, crawls to her mother. She places her hands on Mae/Mother's back, as though to absorb a rogue current that flows through the nakedness, twitching and shuddering all the flesh. The twitching woman dabs at the red tide on her face with skittish fingers, then stares at the splotches of crimson gush on their tips. She looks at her daughter with the pained incomprehension of a wounded animal: the innocence of disbelief. Velvet hugs her mother, burying her face in the bleeding woman's breasts. Fresh cries, softer and more delicate, exhale into the shadows. The young girl with the nail polish flowers on her feet and the Cézanne-bodied woman with the vampy, movie star face fall in tandem to the floor, lie spooning like lovers in the sun on the carpet in the dark hallway.

INT. BRINKLEY'S HELL–MIRROR–
VELVET'S CHILDHOOD HOME–LIVING ROOM–LATER

Velvet sits at a decrepit piano. Her mother enters from the kitchen, drink in hand, wearing a short, silk bathrobe. She has wiped the blood from her swollen face.

MAE/MOTHER

Play for me, darling. Calms me down right away. Oh, wait! Candles, every performance needs candles.

She sets her drink down on a scarred table, spilling a little. As though seized by a sudden fit of amnesia–or merely a leading lady on pause–she is motionless for several moments, before touching her fingers to her brow to channel obscure knowledge through a manicure. Velvet watches her frown and shake her head, then startle as at the blast of a gun.

MAE/MOTHER

Matches . . . matches, matches, matches.

(fishes matches out of a bowl of potpourri)

Aha! Safe, safekeeping.

Several candles stud the room. Mae/Mother attempts to light a match, but her hands are shaking too much.

VELVET

Let me do it.

MAE/MOTHER

No, no, I've got it.

(strikes match)

There. There.

(lights candle, match goes out)

Well. One is all we need.

Retrieves her drink, holds the glass to her face. Looks long at her daughter. Lies down on the floor.

MAE/MOTHER

Okay, I'm ready, darling. Begin. Begin.

Velvet turns to the piano, takes a deep breath, and begins to pick out "Chopsticks." As she plays, her mother cries, and the choking sobs cacophonize with the uncertain musical notes. The song ends and Mae/Mother clamps a hand over her mouth, removes it, breathes deeply and sits up.

MAE/MOTHER

It was an accident. It was an accident. I fell down. He didn't mean . . . It was an accident. Little Vee. My little Vee . . .

Velvet turns and looks at her mother. They stare at one another across the room. The single candle flame unrolls its scarf of smoke, trails its black chiffon through the still air. Velvet nods.

MAE/MOTHER

Oh, you're my little angel. You know that? My little angel. Where's your halo? Your tinfoil halo. I'll make you one tomorrow. I love you, I love only you. Do you know that? Oh, I feel so much better. I feel so much better.

(starts to cry)

So much better. Okay.

(lies down)

I'm just going to lie here for a while. I love it when you play. Calms me down right away. "Play it again, Sam . . ." You know I love *Casablanca*. What a romantic movie.

(laughs bitterly)

"Play it again, Sam . . ."

INT. BRINKLEY'S HELL—MIRROR—
DAVIE'S APARTMENT—BEDROOM—NIGHT

The bedroom walls are overwhelmed by black-and-white posters of Shakespearean stage productions, tiny movie stubs that have been tacked up, random squares of tinfoil, programs from concerts, takeout menus, handwritten lists with headings such as: Things To Do Today, People To Do Today, Things To Do Never, Favourite Words, Words I Hate, Best Hamlets of the Past 100 years, Best Hair in Hollywood, Astrological Combinations Most Often Resulting in True Love, Top Ten Reasons Why There's No Such Thing as True Love, Most Gratifying Sexual Positions/Two Perspectives, Shakespeare's Greatest Tragedies, World's Greatest Poets According To Velvet, Top Seven Reasons Why the Ukulele is the Greatest Instrument on Earth. A bare bulb hangs from the ceiling, while two very phallic-looking lava lamps provide further light. The bed is a mattress on the floor, covered with threadbare and somewhat dirty bedding. The only other furniture in the room is an overturned wooden crate stamped with the words "Produce of Thailand." It serves as a night table, and it is on this that several framed photographs of Velvet—outfitted in elaborate vintage fashion—sit, along with a camera.

Davie is sprawled naked on his bed, smoking a cigarette in an antique cigarette holder. Velvet, clad in hand-painted jeans and a top trimmed with sequins and pink feathers, sits on the bed with her back to a wall, knees drawn chinward, a pillow between her legs. She watches him smoke; her eyes never leave him.

DAVIE

Here.

He passes her the cigarette. She inhales and passes it back to him.

DAVIE

Did you buy me a birthday present?

VELVET

You don't get to know that 'til tomorrow.

DAVIE

Christ got gifts on his birthday.

VELVET

You're not Christ.

DAVIE

How do you know? I could be the Messiah reincarnated, with better hair. Anyway, I deserve a gift. A birthday is a sign of spiritual evolution.

VELVET

How is a birthday a sign of spiritual evolution? It's a sign that you're on a steady march to eventually qualifying for ten percent off the Early Bird Special. And how do you know that Christ got gifts? He wasn't materialistic.

DAVIE

Birthdays create psychological torment. It's the fight against psychological torment that creates spiritual evolution. And I happen to know that all the disciples loved to pool their resources and get JC something special.

VELVET

You're weird. And when have you ever felt psychological torment?

DAVIE

In the lapses between fucking and eating I get a little cranky.

Velvet laughs and touches her feet to Davie's side.

DAVIE

Aaahhh! Your feet are freezing.

VELVET

So pay your heating bills. Then I'd have warm feet.

DAVIE

Don't need to. I'm warm-blooded.

VELVET

I'm not.

DAVIE

It's 'cuz of the straitjacket. It's bad for the circulation.

VELVET

Shut up. I wasn't in a straitjacket—well, not after the first few days. I was in a Quiet Room. But he still came to torture me.

DAVIE

Your friend the Shadowman? Is he still a shape-shifter?

VELVET

He's not my friend. I've never told anyone else about

him, you know. Except for the doctors and they don't believe me, I can tell. They're very condescending.

DAVIE

I believe you, my darling Velcro Chenille. But then, I'm a very deep and sensitive person. If you want my advice, stop telling the doctors that there's a monster-man stalking you, and then you won't have to go to the hospital anymore. I'll keep your secret.

VELVET

But what about when he maims me? He's nice to me sometimes. Sometimes he's fun and creative. He loves movies, all the ones I love. And he's helping me write my book. The meds make me too tired. So I've sort of been forgetting to take them. They make me feel like I'm walking through Jell-O all the time, in slow motion.

DAVIE

Wow, I've never walked through Jell-O in fast motion. That might be a cool feeling.

VELVET

You're not listening. I'm tired of being tired. Everything feels hard. Getting dressed feels hard. And you know what else? I'm afraid he might not come back. Isn't that warped?

DAVIE

No, it's not warped. After all, he knows you so well. But I have a feeling the Shadowman'll be back. Call me psychic. And you know what the Irish say: "The devil you know is better than the devil you don't know." You just happen to have a particularly colourful devil.

VELVET

That's sick.

DAVIE

(shrugs)
You're sick.

Velvet looks wounded.

DAVIE

Relax. I love sick. Sick is beautiful. Sick is interesting.

VELVET

Will you come visit me in the Quiet Room?

DAVIE

I always come visit you. Since when would I ever pass up the opportunity to give my two cents' worth of advice to the medical establishment?

VELVET

I wish I were more like you.

DAVIE

Charming and devilishly handsome? My darling, there is only so much charisma to go around.

Davie balances the cigarette holder on an empty tuna can on the crate-cum-night table. He holds out his arms to Velvet.

DAVIE

Princess Velcro Chenille!

Velvet tosses the pillow she held between her legs and dives on top of Davie, giggling.

VELVET

Squeeze me. Who do you love most in the world?

DAVIE

Velcro Chenille.

VELVET

How do I know for sure?

DAVIE

Have I fucked you lately?

VELVET

No.

DAVIE

There you go. I don't fuck people I love.

VELVET

So that leaves how many?

DAVIE

You and . . . you.
(laughs)
Love is highly overrated.

VELVET

It's natural. Part of life.

DAVIE

Ah yes, but life is the most unnatural of states. It offends the very core of being!

VELVET

What dead Germanic philosopher are you channelling?

DAVIE

I only speak the truth—the cosmic truth. So if life is unnatural then love, as a part of life, must also be deemed unnatural, or, rather, severely out of place.

VELVET

But you love me.

DAVIE

Did I say that? Yeah, well. A performance, darling,

it's all a performance. God's a recidivist. He likes to watch reruns.

(screams at the ceiling)

Time for a hiatus! I'm fucking sick of this! I want a new trailer!

Several moments of silence.

DAVIE

(to Velvet)

He's in a production meeting.

(yells at the ceiling)

I know how this movie ends!

Again, silence.

VELVET

I thought you were an atheist.

DAVIE

Depends on my mood. Which depends on my blood sugar. So really my entire spiritual ethos is based around insulin.

Velvet rolls off the bed and begins perusing the selection of takeout menus pinned to the walls.

VELVET

So are we ordering in? Agnostic pizza, reincarnated Pad Thai, Godless sashimi?

DAVIE

You can if you want. I'm going out. Save some for me.

VELVET

Where're you going?

DAVIE

The witching hour nears. I'm off to get myself a little warlock for my birthday.

He moves to get off the bed. Velvet sets a new land-speed record charging from a menu to Davie's feet. She grabs his arm.

VELVET

Stay. Stay. Stay. Stay. Stay.

DAVIE

Five stays. Not enough for a corset, my dear, though you're starting to need one.

VELVET

Cruel.

DAVIE

Yeah.

VELVET

Stay.

DAVIE

No.

Velvet continues to cling to his arm. He tries to shake her off. They end up wrestling on the floor.

VELVET

(crying)

You promised! You promised! Don't go!

DAVIE

Fuck off! Fuck you! Get off me!

He manages to pin her to the floor.

DAVIE

(screams into her face)

Stop it! Stop! Stop!

Velvet's struggles chameleon into limp surrender, and a moment ices over in stillness between them.

DAVIE

(speaks slowly)

I will be back late. If you're here, you better not be alone. You better be in the company of cold egg rolls. Nod if you understand me.

She nods. He slips his tongue into her mouth, a silky probe that mines deep. Her body buckles and shakes.

INT. BRINKLEY'S HELL—MIRROR—
DAVIE'S APARTMENT—BATHROOM—LATER

Velvet stands before the toothpaste-speckled mirror. Shy, uncertain fingers discover the skin of her face. She does not see her reflection.

INT. BRINKLEY'S HELL—MIRROR—
DAVIE'S BATHROOM—MIRROR—CONTINUOUS

The Shadowman appears. He is styled as a Gene Kelly look-alike, a lá *Singin' in the Rain*, and his yellow raincoat is painfully shiny. A smile, like the ripples from a plunged stone, radiates across his face. He opens a bright yellow umbrella.

SHADOWMAN

Is it rainin'? Are you sad? Did the motherfucker leave you again? There, there, pet. I'll cheer you up in a jiffy. Shall we sing a song? Can you tap dance? Take my hand. I'll show you how.

He extends his hand to her while twirling the umbrella over his head. His eyes gleam and his teeth twinkle.

**INT. BRINKLEY'S HELL—MIRROR—
DAVIE'S BATHROOM—CONTINUOUS**

Velvet's eyes shoot joyful sparklers of recognition into the movie star gaze in the mirror. She shrieks and giggles like a child sprayed by a hose on a hot day, and begins to belt out "Singin' in the Rain."

**INT. BRINKLEY'S HELL—MIRROR—
DAVIE'S BATHROOM—MIRROR—CONTINUOUS**

The Shadowman—as Gene Kelly—is tap dancing as though he's got hot coals in his shoes. Wild acrobatic leaps and twirls of his umbrella fill up his silvery stage. His eyes glitter, splintered with diamond chips of mischief. He pauses and steps to the fore, not in the least out of breath. The yellow umbrella gives his face a jaundiced look.

SHADOWMAN

Did you put your dancing shoes on?

He tosses the umbrella and holds out his arms.

SHADOWMAN

(urgently)

Jump into my arms! Jump into my arms! Dance with me!

**INT. BRINKLEY'S HELL—MIRROR—
DAVIE'S BATHROOM—CONTINUOUS**

Shattered glass covers the bathroom and Velvet like lethal, oversized snowflakes. She is on the floor, a tassel of blood streaming from a small gash near her eye. Her fingers smudge the crimson into sponge art. The canvas of her face is dazed, unable to comprehend the colour it has been splashed with, or why.

The Shadowman steps from the corner of the room. He no longer looks like Gene Kelly. His face is painted white, with two red streaks running down from his coal-black eyes. He is dressed all in black, but his feet are bare. His nails are painted black, and long and pointed as fangs.

SHADOWMAN

Oopsie-daisy! What happened, my pet? Not much of a dancer, are you?

Glass crunches beneath his feet like eggshells, but he does not bleed. Spears of clarity and comprehension shoot through Velvet's daze; she trembles. A whimper escapes her throat, sirens into a keening scream. A black-nailed hand smacks her face silent. Then that same hand picks up a large shard of glass, places it with great ceremony on Velvet's crimsoned palm.

SHADOWMAN

Here you go, little girl. Here you go.

INT. BRINKLEY'S HELL—MIRROR—
DAVIE'S APARTMENT—BATHROOM—DAWN

Davie pushes open the bathroom door, rubbing his face. For a moment he freezes at the sight of bloody Velvet on the floor, her body surrounded by the jagged remains of the mirror. Then he is with her, cradling her head.

DAVIE

Velvet! Velvet! Fuck . . .

Velvet opens her eyes, focuses and smiles. Her smile is shoved aside by deep lines of worry.

VELVET

What's wrong? What happened?

DAVIE

Fuck me.

He helps her sit up and she looks around with wide, baffled eyes.

VELVET

What? Did you? I . . .

Davie examines her left wrist, which is covered in dried blood.

DAVIE

Look at you. Oh, Vee.

He rummages through the cabinet, tossing nail polish remover, a makeup kit, a blonde wig, box of condoms and a screwdriver onto the floor. He unearths a towel and soaks it under the faucet. Velvet continues to slump against the side of the bathtub, eyes glossy with bewilderment. Davie crouches beside her and wipes at her wrist, hurried but gentle.

DAVIE

Goddamn it. I must've been Florence Fucking Nightingale in a former life. Hmmm . . . that could be an idea for a new drag act. You're my inspiration, Velcro Chenille.

VELVET

Florence Nightingale?

Davie's eyes are lush with tears.

DAVIE

Oh, babe. Well, it's not too deep. You missed all the big veins. Your aim is for shit.

He begins to wipe the dried blood from her face and hands.

DAVIE

Scared the hell outta me.

VELVET

Sorry.

DAVIE

My fast food-fed heart can't take it.

INT. BRINKLEY'S HELL—MIRROR—
DAVIE'S BEDROOM—A SHORT TIME LATER

Velvet and Davie are on his bed. He is wrapping her wrist in an entire roll of gauze. Her hands are covered in "Van Gogh's 'Starry Night' Band-Aids."

VELVET

Sorry about your mirror.

DAVIE

(winks)

That's okay. Now I don't have to clean it! Not that I was going to.

VELVET

I don't really remember. He was dancing . . .

Davie places his hand over her mouth.

DAVIE

Miss Florence is in the building! She'd probably sing a lullaby, wouldn't she? I don't know any. Oh wait, yes I do.

(sings)

"Twinkle twinkle, little star . . ."

"Wee Willie Winkie runs through the town, upstairs and downstairs in his nightgown . . ." That's more like a rhyme.

VELVET

It's okay. Don't sing.

DAVIE

Or you'll slice up your other wrist?

VELVET

(chuckles)

Something like that.

DAVIE

Velvet, don't ever do that again. Or I'll have to kill you.

VELVET

Promise?

DAVIE

You wanna go back to the Cracker Farm?

VELVET

No. But you'll come visit me, right? You always do. He's gone now . . . the Shadowman. Skedaddled. But he'll be back. He always comes back. I'm so tired.

(pause)

Did you find a warlock?

DAVIE

Two. Ha ha! Happy Birthday to me.

VELVET

Yeah. Happy Birthday. It's official. Davie?

DAVIE

Yeah?

They stare at one another for a long time, as though waiting for something to break the surface of the gaze. Velvet shrugs. Davie nods.

VELVET

I'm hungry.

DAVIE

Me too.

He touches her face, near the gash by her eye.

DAVIE

Guess there's no cold egg rolls, huh?

Dear Velvet,

No, I was not a drag queen. (Pity, that. Who can deny that they are the best performers in the world?) Nor did I own a doll collection. (I am afraid of dolls. They have empty eyes.) I am not gay. (Does sexual orientation still exist in Hell? One would assume so, since it makes much of life Hell—why not continue the torment? And if phone sex is possible, then letter sex must be possible, too. Not that I am thinking we are going to have letter sex. Ignore that. Freudian slip. Someone should really have killed Freud sooner.) It is just that I have always admired the bias-cut dress. So I owned a few. My mother had a marvellous sense of style. And there is nothing quite like peach angora. Indeed, I do feel a real kinship with the film director Ed Wood. It's like you already know everything about me. I find your understanding of me very touching.

My mirror has gone fuzzy and staticky, like a broken television set, or one whose power source is in doubt. It crackles, full of black and white electronic-type snow. But then a channel will come in quite suddenly, so to speak, as though a Great Plug has been adjusted and the show goes on. I believe . . . how do I say this . . . that the movie I have glimpsed is comprised of scenes from your life. I saw a little girl, a pale, lissome version of the beautiful woman—you—I first saw in my mirror. You were with your mother (?)—I was given only snatches—at any rate, the little girl was with a woman who looks like Mae West, a dark-haired Mae West. And then there was a man, a Greek-looking man, and he and Mae were together, and then he fled in an angry flurry . . . and the child saw everything. I am sorry. Help me understand what I see. More electronic blizzard obscured all images, and then I saw you—it could not have been a picture from all that long ago—with a young man: curly-haired, sensual, irregular features. Your paramour? There was a fight and he left. And then you were alone in a bathroom staring into the mirror. I caught a glimpse of a man in a yellow raincoat who looked like Gene Kelly—though there was something menacing about him. Static broke the scene again and when the picture returned you were on the bathroom floor, covered in glass and blood. You screamed in terror and then went silent as a shadow. You picked up a shard of glass and sliced at your wrist. More static. And then the young man walked into the bathroom and cradled your head. Am I watching your life, or are my eyes watching some devilish invention? If it be the truth—or even if not—I am compelled now to confess to you all of myself as it existed, with no embellishment, and to undo untruths, including minor ones.

I have lied to you. I am sorry. I promise I will not lie to you anymore. I admit I feel ridiculous to have lied, and I do not possess the requisite suave to gracefully—or satisfactorily—explain why. I am not sure that I know why. The truth seems rather bendable in here, or it did until I bent it and was wracked by terrible remorse. Fibbing (such a harmless-sounding word, isn't it?) to you makes it feel as though the walls are closing in on me. I had never associated guilt with claustrophobia before. If there is further Judgment awaiting us, I hope this does not affect my case. I guess you think I am kind of pathetic, lying in Hell? But old habits die hard. And I have found that if you tell yourself something enough times, it becomes a reasonable approximation of the truth.

I am not a banker. I am a file clerk at a plastics company. But had I not been run over, I might have been a banker: in the moments before I died, I was on my way to apply for a job as a Customer Service Representative at a very large bank. Normally, I have a problem with touching money, but my doctor had given me some pills that seemed to help and I was excited about trying this new thing. You know, facing fears.

There was nothing drastically wrong with my job as a file clerk. It was mindless enough to let me think about whatever I wanted. Intellectual freedom is found in odd places. I have a talent for organizing and I think I improved on their system quite a bit. Really, the company would not have run so smoothly without me. I was the nuts and bolts of that operation. But nobody ever realized, much less said thank you. Credit never goes where credit is due, does it?

The thing that I liked about my job, other than the fact that it came with dental, was the sense of calm the act of filing brought me. I was very tense when I first started, of course, but once I had mastered—in fact, developed—the system, I was free to think about other things. I liked to recite poetry to myself as I filed, especially "The Passionate Shepherd to His Love." A flawless lyric. I love Marlowe. Literature is full of romantic figures, but to me he is unsurpassed. I used to have fantasies about dying in a tavern brawl. But if you are not leaving anything brilliant behind, what is the point? There is something very disconcerting about outliving your idol—turning thirty was depressing, to say the least. Once I was older than he was when he died—Marlowe having achieved immortality as a great writer—I felt like a dusty relic, and the years stretched out flat and endless while my capacity for greatness seemed to shrink to the point of invisibility. It certainly did not help that Rudolph Valentino—another idol of mine—died at thirty-one. I must say I found that my thirties in general were nothing to write home about.

I do not know if I would have been very good in a bank. To be honest, even if I had gotten an interview, I do not think I would have tried for it. Sometimes receiving the invitation is enough—actually attending the party is like one too many icing roses on an already sweet cake. It is very stressful to be on your feet talking to people all day, and as I mentioned, handling money is difficult for me. There are a lot of germs on the faces of those dead Prime Ministers, not to mention the Queen.

Anyway, as I walked along that day, on my way to submit my resumé, I was feeling bolder and happier than usual. It was a Friday, and I had called in sick. I always go to the same café at 8:43 A.M. Punctuality is a virtue. Everyone there knows me, and they let me bring my own mug, since I prefer not to use drinking vessels belonging to others, even if they are single-use paper cups. Who knows, I may have landed an interview! But I guess that information will be forever kept from me.

Again, I am sorry I lied.

While I am apologizing, I feel that I must also say that I am sorry about my appearance, in case it disappointed you. Perhaps this sounds strange, but I was initially terrified that you saw me, terrified and disappointed. Somehow it seemed easier to write to you knowing that you had no idea what I looked like. But now I want you to see me. Although I cannot stop myself from writing apologetic rambles like this one. So: sorry that my nose and chin are unevenly distributed. And it has been proven beyond a reasonable doubt, as you saw, that I will not develop shoulders before I die. I know that—unless things have altered in your room—you have no one else to correspond with. Nevertheless, I hope that my person did not disappoint. No one likes to be chosen by default.

Shut up, Brinkley. Is that what you are thinking? Once one embarks on a tangent rife with worries, it is difficult to reset the course. Next topic: I suppose the fact that I am not actually a banker has rearranged your ideas about what kind of place I lived in. It was a very nice, thoroughly disinfected basement suite, in an older but very nice house. Actually, my mother lived in the house; I rented the basement from her. She has been sick the last few years and I was trying to take care of her. It was a brown house with large hedges in front, and two prominent upstairs windows that looked like eyes. My suite was small, but it had hardwood floors, like yours, and bright warm yellow walls, just like Monet's dining room at Giverny. I did not have any Monet poster prints, but I had a Matisse, the one with the wild dancers that caused a critic to label him a Fauve. (What do critics know, anyway?) I also had a Chagall, "Bouquet with Flying Lovers." And three de Lempickas. I loved Degas, too. All that tulle is beautiful to me. And of course, I had lots of pictures of Clara Bow, my favourite actress. Do you have favourite artists?

I had a small closet that I kept very organized with a special system that I invented, which sorted things based on colour and the type of buttons on any given garment. I had fourteen suits that I wore to work, according to my work-wardrobe rotation schedule. I did not really have to wear a suit to work, there was no rule saying that the file clerk had to wear a tie, but I always felt more ready to face the world in a suit. I found that the right tie was a sort of armour. Somehow, I believe you understand my meaning.

I went around the corner to a tiny diner every day to eat my meals; the people were very nice and got to know me. Restaurants are a great breeding ground for bacteria, but this one was particularly clean and I felt comfortable there. The owner's name was Mary and she was very good to me. She was a great fan of silent films and we would have long conversations about the nuances of old cinema. She loved Valentino. I never ate in any other restaurant. I always brought something home for my mother to eat, usually macaroni and cheese or chicken soup.

So, like you, I have left my mother behind. I miss her, of course, although in the last few years we had not spoken all that much—I mentioned to you that she had not been very well. I worry about who will take care of her. My aunt lives in Boston; maybe she will have to come and stay. My father left when I was a baby, and disappeared. I don't mean literally, I am sure he is around somewhere, but I never saw him, so consequently I do not miss him now. You have not mentioned your father. Where is he? I did not have many friends, either—what do they call us, lone wolves?

No, Velvet, I do not think anyone hates you. Certainly not your mother, nor your friend Davie. They love you and they understand. I must say—and please do not take this the wrong way—I admire you. I admit there were moments, while I was filing or at night alone with Clara Bow, in which I thought of doing what you did, but I never had the courage. I think you are very brave. I do not know, Velvet, how we are going to carry on here. We have been awaiting the Judgment, but perhaps this is it. You are right that the weight of missing someone, of absence, crushes—so many moments I feel as if I cannot breathe in and out one more time. I do not suppose we can die all over again; if we did it would likely be just another step on the treadmill that would return us to this place. (Always hated repetitive cardio.) I will tell you a secret: I do not have too many people to long for. I am longing for the familiar, for the sounds my house made at night, for lying in bed listening to horns on the street, for macaroni and cheese and lattes with soymilk, for my bedroom and my clothes, and most of all for Clara Bow. I am longing to see you. But I guess, to keep breathing in and out, we write letters and wait. There must be more to this place, Velvet. And I am here, thinking of you, on the other side of the wall.

Yours very truly,
Brinkley

He saw my life, he saw my life, he saw my life.... A clump of words repeated over and over lose all semantics, become instead a pulsing sensate clot. There was no mistaking what he had described, so great was the feeling of my skin being peeled away and the salty pour of memories attacking the rawness. Yet I was surprised by my lack of shame in light of Brinkley's innocent voyeurism. There was more a rueful smile, a shrugging of the shoulders.

How many men (straight ones) have even heard of Clara Bow, let alone love her? How many actually like silent movies? How many understand the protective force of a good tie? Far too few, in my book.

And what he said in answer to my question about whether I am hated made me feel a little better. Perhaps completely untrue, but kind of him to say.

I looked out the barred window at the visual equivalent of white noise. Not mist, fog, smoke or snow, but pure matterless white. There was an opaque quality to it, so despite its natural bright, it didn't hurt my eyes. There was a tearing sensation, though, in my chest, a ripped-at-the-roots hollow. I pushed forward and leaned low over the desk, on my elbows, and pressed my face between the bars to the window, unloosing my squashed kiss against the chill glass. My breath bloomed a flower.

Did he really say he admired me?

Hot pink eyeshade was pushed up on my head, so when I looked in the mirror I had two sets of eyes. One, headlight-sized and blinkless, with braidable lashes; the other, large-lidded and shiny, and steadily turning colour. The blue outline had grown and was encroaching ever more on the blacky-brown, though not in any neatly defined way. There was no tidy border now, the sapphire ring a wavy ellipse, one colour spilling over the other. It gave my eye an odd marbled effect. I imagined Brinkley's eyes looking the same way, except a spillage of blue and green. I wished I could see them for real.

So where was *my* movie? I peered at the glass hard, until my eyes felt as though they glowed with the effort. And like a snake willed by the desire of its charmer, my reflection was gradually obscured by an electronic blizzard.

INT. VELVET'S HELL—MIRROR—
BRINKLEY'S CHILDHOOD HOME—BATHROOM—NIGHT

Brinkley sits on the bathroom floor picking lint out of the valleys between his toes. He is a young boy.

His mother relaxes in the bathtub. She bears an uncanny resemblance to Rita Hayworth. Her feet are thrown over the edge of the tub, glistening with damp and their own incandescent pallor. She smokes with one hand while the other lithe arm uncoils from her chest and extends into the air holding aloft a glass of clear liquid, a sliding mirror ruled by the minute inflections of her wrist. She stares at it, eye to a crystal ball, on the hunt for her reflection, or the future.

RITA/MOTHER

Baby. BABY.

Brinkley stops arranging his lint balls into a star pattern on the tile, and looks up. Rita/Mother unlooses a giggle that touches off a chain of hiccups. The hiccups alternate with giggles until both are lost to a maelstrom of ragged coughs. Her small son sits in silence, Argus-eyed.

RITA/MOTHER

Fucking Mother of God.

Once the hacking subsides, the clear liquid in the glass obeys the motion of her hand, rushes to the rim and over, the necessary tonic down her throat. After she swallows, Rita/Mother gazes into the empty glass for what seems to her son a long time, her siren loveliness cataloguing a baffled gravity.

RITA/MOTHER

Oh-oh.

Laughter once again overtakes her, deeper and louder than before, its hollow bell tolling in every corner of the bathroom. Choking coughs displace the bell and Rita/Mother contorts as though she may retch a lung. A clot of jellied yellow emerges from her mouth and plops into the glass. She groans and sets her cup of biology on the edge of the tub, leans her head back and slides further into the water. A come-hither mask obscures her features and she starts to belt out "Put the Blame on Mame" from the Rita Hayworth film *Gilda*.

Brinkley/Argus is motionless, taking his place alongside ancient gods in his all-seeing sweep of vision. Rita/ Mother stops singing mid-song, arches her back, shakes her mane and sighs. Her long-fingered hands cup her breasts, push them chinward. She appears to be testing them out, searching for something. A sudden racket of sloshing water, up and over its white cage—the flame-headed mermaid is face-to-face with her child. She blows smoke.

RITA/MOTHER

(low)

What happened to you?

(louder)

What happened to you?

Brinkley's arms are wrapped around his legs, rendering him a tight ball of boy, and he looks up into the two lights for eyes that blaze down at him.

RITA/MOTHER

Are you deaf? Are you an idiot? Did I give birth to an idiot?

She falls back into the water with a cry.

RITA/MOTHER

(low)

Twit.

(then, to herself)

Where's my daughter?

Sobs fill up the bathroom, plangent with phlegm. Up pops the mermaid's head, her arms reaching over the edge of the tub, fingers stretched and taut with desperation.

RITA/MOTHER

ComehereI'msorryI'msorryI'msorrybeautifulbeautiful mylittleboy!

The long fingers make a grab for Brinkley, pull him into

soaking breasts, bury his face. She rocks him, strokes his hair.

RITA/MOTHER

Mommy loves you. Mommy loves you so much. You're my boy.

Draws back suddenly, jerked by a string. Eyes orbed with strange light, fantastical fairy flame like her hair.

RITA/MOTHER

Don't you leave me. Promise me you won't leave me. Okay? Promise? Promise me?

Brinkley nods, face bearing the grave frown of a grave covenant. The mermaid takes his face in her hands, runs her prune-y fingers down his cheeks.

RITA/MOTHER

You are such a good boy. You're the best boy in the whole world.

(to herself)

But I want my little girl.

The good little boy watches as Aphrodite of the nether regions rises, sans seashell, from her murky, shallow sea. Water streams from her pubic hair, limp locks spill pell-mell over her shoulders, stick to her breasts like seaweed.

RITA/MOTHER

Darling, hand me a towel.

Brinkley obliges, and Rita/Mother lights up like a Christmas tree, drops her cigarette in the bath.

RITA/MOTHER

Oh my God, Brinkley!

(lets towel fall in water)

Oh my God! I have the best idea!

INT. VELVET'S HELL—MIRROR—BRINKLEY'S CHILDHOOD HOME—LIVING ROOM—A SHORT TIME LATER

Rita/Mother wears a red silk robe that bears a sinister dragon on the back. It keeps falling open. Together, she and Brinkley have pulled all the cushions off the living room couch and chairs, and are stacking them to make a fort. A bounty of blankets is at the ready to make a roof. Brinkley stacks the cushions, paying special attention to the matching up of edges, sure and sober of face, and doesn't look up when his mother flies from the room.

RITA/MOTHER

I want potato chips! Brinkley, do you want to make pancakes? Let's have pancakes in our fort!

He hears the pour of popcorn kernels and a few minutes later they pop to life, a blitz of tiny gunshots.

RITA/MOTHER

Did you eat all the pickles?

BRINKLEY

(to himself)

I don't like pickles.

Rita/Mother begins to sing "My Funny Valentine" at the top of her lungs. She gets to "Your looks are laughable" and then stops, charges into the living room and stands stock-still, staring at Brinkley.

RITA/MOTHER

I'm bored. Let's play dress-up. And I have to finish my goddamn painting! I can't work like this!

She rushes from the room. Brinkley shakes out a blanket, prepares to lay the roof on his fort. He is methodical, seemingly insensible to his mother's manic behaviour.

Minutes later, Rita/Mother appears in the doorway that hinges kitchen to living room, poses with one arm high above her head, a cigarette in hand. A full, white breast slips free, gleams in the lamplight. In her other hand, she clutches a bag full of clothes.

RITA/MOTHER

Oh my darling. You are so beautiful.

Strides across the room, red hair and red silk flying.

RITA/MOTHER

(drops the bag, cigarette hanging from her lips)

Dance with me.

Brinkley is smothered by giggles and hair, dropping the roof of the fort as he is dragged 'round the room in a quasi-tango, 'til his mother trips and they both take headers into the pile of cushions that he had so carefully arranged. Laughter from the dancers hits the four walls of the room; the woman's is loud and infectious, and her small son rides on it like a raft. It takes him in, as her arms open and she draws the bony boy to her skin, and he lies in a heady cloud of gin and lavender perfume. After a moment she pushes him away, leaps up and moves to a corner of the room. Pulls a sheet off an easel upon which sits a large canvas, a vivid unfinished abstract of a small boy with multiple sets of eyes.

RITA/MOTHER

Do you like this? I'm getting mixed signals.

BRINKLEY

What is it?

RITA/MOTHER

How should I know? I just paint what I'm told.

BRINKLEY

Who tells you?

RITA/MOTHER

The Committee. You know, they tell everyone what to do. Especially artists. Because we know the secret code.

(indicating painting)

Yes, this one is going to be special.

BRINKLEY

(nods solemnly)

Special.

Rita/Mother flings her arms around him, biting his ear.

RITA/MOTHER

Mommy loves you, Mommy loves you, Mommy loves you!

BRINKLEY

Ow!

He tries to protect his ear. She draws back as though shot through with electricity.

RITA/MOTHER

Promise me. Promise me you'll never leave.

BRINKLEY

I promise. But no biting.

RITA/MOTHER

Pinky swear.

Brinkley holds up his little pinky and his mother entwines it in her own.

RITA/MOTHER

That means we'll be together forever.

A blizzard of sloppy kisses; a belch escapes her throat. Brinkley wipes his face. The belcher laughs.

RITA/MOTHER

What's that smell? Oh my God, the popcorn!

Shuttles at star-speed from the room, while Brinkley scrubs his cheek with a wool blanket. Appears in the doorway, glistening lips in a mock-pout and a drink in her hand.

RITA/MOTHER

I burned it.

(exiting back into kitchen)

Wine gums, wine gums, salt water taffy, where's my record player?

She returns, picks up the bag of clothes, rummages.

RITA/MOTHER

Dress-up time my angel! Where's my goddamn red lipstick?

BRINKLEY

I don't want to. I'm tired.

RITA/MOTHER

Nonsense! I want my little girl! I want my goddamn . . . Am I wearing any lipstick? Did I forget?

She blots her mouth with her fingers, checking for colour. Pulls a gold tube of red lipstick out of the dress-up bag.

RITA/MOTHER

Ah, my magic wand!

(smears her lips, smacks them together)

Much better, my darling, much better. I need my red armour. And so do you! Come, come.

Brinkley shakes his head and turns away. Rita/Mother grabs him, points the tube of lipstick like a gun.

RITA/MOTHER

Assume the position.

He shakes his head, mouth set in a steely line. She grabs his face, squishes his mouth into a pout and smudges it red like a child playing with crayons, colouring outside the lines. Brinkley struggles and whimpers.

RITA/MOTHER

Stay still! You're ruining my work.

(inspecting his face)

There. Very pretty. What a pretty little thing you are. Now—your outfit. You simply can't go to Sing Sing with a green face! Ha! Remember that movie, darling? Weren't the clothes divine? Oh, I could be happy if I lived in a movie like that, couldn't I? Let's live together in a movie, my angel, shall we? We'd be happy then, I know we would.

She rifles through the bag, pulling out clothing and tossing it about. Out comes a frilly peach-coloured little girl's dress and a white satin evening gown. Rita/Mother drops her robe and stands naked before her son, touching the white satin to her cheek. Brinkley looks away.

RITA/MOTHER

Oh darling, it's so beautiful. I live for beauty! Do you think I should paint in this dress? Inspiring, no? You can't feel sad in a dress like this, angel. It's not possible!

She slips it on, struts about the room, strikes a pose.

RITA/MOTHER

Okay darling, now it's your turn! Everyone gets a turn to be beautiful! That's what The Committee always says!

Brinkley backs away, but she grabs him and pulls off his clothes. He shivers, shoulders hunched. She pulls the little dress over his head, does up the sash.

RITA/MOTHER

Oh, spin 'round for me! Let me look at you!

Brinkley is motionless, staring at the floor. Rita/Mother gently lifts his chin.

RITA/MOTHER

Mommy loves you. You are so pretty.

She smiles softly, her mania seeming to dissipate. He smiles back, reaches out and touches her hair.

RITA/MOTHER

You're beautiful, just like my little girl that died.

BRINKLEY

What little girl?

RITA/MOTHER

My little girl. She died. And then I got you.

BRINKLEY

Are you sad?

RITA/MOTHER

Yes, sometimes I'm sad. But I love to see you in her dress. It makes me happy.

(pause)

Oh! I know what would make me happy—a snack! Let's have a little tea party, darling!

She bolts into the kitchen. Surveying the ruination of the would-be fort, Brinkley appears to consider—for an instant—taking up the cause again, stacking the cushions, matching up the edges, choosing a blanket to keep out the rain. But exhaustion knocks him into a little ball on the floor, half-covered by a pilled green throw. A train of spittle has chugged its way down Brinkley's chin by the time the lady in white shakes him awake, a new drink in hand.

RITA/MOTHER

BrinkleyBrinkleyBrinkley! I found my record player.

Oh my God—the moon, have you seen the moon? It's beautiful, it's beautiful, come look, come look, come look!

BRINKLEY

(drowsily)

Mommy. Tired.

Out on the porch she goes, letting a frigid squall dervish through the front door and around the living room. Brinkley wipes his eyes and sits up, squinting, cuddles the throw to his chest. He drags it behind him when he gets up and goes after his mother.

INT. VELVET'S HELL—MIRROR—
EXT. BRINKLEY'S CHILDHOOD HOME—PORCH—CONTINUOUS

She's naked in the glow of the porch light: drink in one hand, cigarette in the other, dress at her feet.

BRINKLEY

(trying to cover her with blanket)

Mommy, it's cold!

One hand pushes him away, the other raises her glass as though toasting the sky. She blows smoke at the moon.

RITA/MOTHER

Oh baby, look at that. It's so gorgeous, it's so gorgeous!

The moon is full, the kind of full that makes it look as though it could split the seam of sky that surrounds it, the kind of full that makes a tunnel of glow into which one might disappear. Rita/Mother takes a drink and wipes her mouth, stands as though before a prophet at whose feet she may lay her life.

RITA/MOTHER

See that man! See that man up there! He works for The Committee.

(yelling at the moon)

I need to finish my goddamn painting! Tell me what to do!

Her face is a canvas of wild mania underpainted with the beauty of her face. Brinkley takes her hand.

BRINKLEY

Mommy, come inside! You'll get sick!

RITA/MOTHER

(calling)

Hello! Down here!

A wave of the arms sends a slosh from the glass onto the porch and Brinkley's small cold foot.

RITA/MOTHER

He doesn't live in a cheese house. Only stupid people think that. Oh, look! He can see us! Hello!

(running onto the lawn)

Hello!

Brinkley panics and takes off after her down the porch steps, scanning the dark street to see who might be staring at this naked woman and her frilly-dressed little boy. By the time his feet hit the wet grass she's dancing Fauvishly, homage to Matisse. Her drink-free hand runs itself over her breasts again and again; her hips draw figure eights on the night. The moon is so huge that it does seem, for an instant, that it might see the echoing white lavishness of one of its disciples swirling on a patch of city grass. Brinkley tries to block her from view of the street, spreading his bony, loose-jointed arms wide, stretching them so taut that his elbows bend backward.

RITA/MOTHER

(yells)

You look like a scarecrow!

The dancing woman spins around the yard, dropping her empty glass and tossing her cigarette as she goes. The little bodyguard running after her slips on the cold dew and falls, starts to cry. He gets back up and launches at Rita/Fauve, grabs her 'round the waist, holds fast.

BRINKLEY

(cries)

Mommy, stop! Come inside!

The dancer picks up her son, squeezes him hard and laughs.

RITA/MOTHER

Inside! Inside! He always wants to go inside! Yes, boss.

(stumbling onto porch)

My little love, my little love! You're bloody heavy!

The bloody heavy little boy is dropped with a thud on the porch, and his mother twirls into the house. He picks up the white dress that lies near the doormat. Brinkley spots the dropped glass on the lawn as he glances back. Stutter-stepping, he thinks to retrieve it, but his feet tingling with cold carry him into the house and he slams the door.

INT. VELVET'S HELL—MIRROR—BRINKLEY'S CHILDHOOD HOME—RITA/MOTHER'S BEDROOM—A SHORT TIME LATER

Rita/Mother and Brinkley are huddled in bed. She is nude; he is clad in underwear. The peach-coloured little dress he wore earlier lies discarded on the floor.

RITA/MOTHER

Tell me a story.

Sleep keeps jerking Brinkley's eyelids as if they're Venetian blinds, but his mother won't stop talking and he's shaking with cold too much to retreat into dreams.

RITA/MOTHER

I'll tell a story! You're so boring.

Up she pops and into the middle of the mattress, jumping like mad. Brinkley struggles to sit up, rubbing his eyes. He stares up at his beautiful mother, at the ostentatious flopping of her hair and body.

RITA/MOTHER

(yells)

Brinkley, jump with me!

The little boy is dragged to his feet, puppeteered from one corner of the bed to another. Rita/Mother laughs and laughs, her mouth an insane half-moon upon her face. Brinkley starts to giggle too, looking up at her wild light-burst eyes. She stops jumping and strikes a pose, leans like the Tower of Pisa and crumples face-first into the pillows, springs back up and takes the floor, arms spread wide. Her son collapses to the bed and pulls his knees to his chest, watching.

RITA/MOTHER

Once upon a time, there was a beautiful young woman.

(pause, fixes hair)

What was her name? Gilda. That's a pretty name. Love that movie. I could've been an actress. But . . .

(drifts off)

What was I saying? Oh, you wanted a story. A young woman . . . This woman was so beautiful that everyone stared when she walked down the street. Then one day, this woman met a handsome young man. And they had a baby—or was it two? And then one day he left. Disappeared.

(pause)

Why?

Arms drop to her sides.

RITA/MOTHER

Fuck that. I hate that story. Where's my happy ending? Where's my little girl? Do you know what happens to people when they die? I want to know.

Once again her son is bounced as she leaps onto the bed, grabs him by the shoulders, moves her nose to his.

RITA/MOTHER

You're my little girl now. Brinkley, I want a happy ending.

There is a sudden stillness in the room, an intake of breath. The boy wiggles his lashes in hers, a butterfly kiss. He stares at cat's eye glimmer, lash-swept and lucent. Pounce! goes the feline, tickle go Brinkley's feet. She's got them in her long white hands.

RITA/MOTHER

"This little piggy went to market, this little piggy stayed home. This little piggy had roast beef for dinner, this little piggy had none. And this little piggy cried wee wee wee wee all the way home!"

Brinkley squeals with laughter and his mother squeals too, and they both fall into goose down. Rita/Mother grabs his face and presses her mouth hard on his. Then she curves away, hands pressed to her face, and sobs. Brinkley sits up, touches his mouth. He places his hands on his mother's back. She leaps to a wall, faces her son with one trembling finger pointed.

RITA/MOTHER

Fuck you. Fuck you. Fuck you. Fuck you. Fuck you.

Slides and curls, a fetal-corpse on the floor. Brinkley curls on the bed. Minutes fall away in the dark vacuum of a bedroom in a house in a city in the middle of the night, and through his tears this small boy watches his mother's wracked form on the floor. He wipes his face but the tears keep coming, and he makes a slow brave crawl off the bed and across to the heap of fairy-haired, siren-bodied woman. When he gets close enough to touch her, he stops. He doesn't put out a hand, keeps both over his crying mouth. In a moment she unfurls, streaming eyes blinking as at a new world. She snatches up her boy, presses him to her chest as if trying to absorb the little body through her skin, into her heart.

RITA/MOTHER

Don't go. Don't go.

Dear Brinkley,

There's a movie in my mirror too! Scenes shown with great clarity out of storms of electronic snow. I saw a goddess-type woman, a Rita Hayworth look-alike, and her young son. You and your mother. The little boy had your same sad, clear eyes. The enthusiastic opening of this letter belies the sadness of what I saw. Your mother screamed at the moon. And at her son: you. I'm sorry. Was she always crazy? And did she always dress you up like a girl? Tell me more.

Yes, it could only have been my mother and me that you saw. I don't think I want you to see any more. But, then again, maybe I do. I have nothing else to give you. (It's a sad moment when you realize that all you have to give is a movie of your life, and it's probably not even a good movie. First-time director, a few arthouse touches, questionable acting—eventually relegated to an existentially dusty corner of a video store. Great wardrobe, though.) Funny, you noticed right away that she looked like Mae West. She liked men. What can I say? She liked food, too. Great taste in one, but not in the other.

A little confused about the fact that you're not gay, or a drag queen. I guess this would be confirmed, as far as it is able to be confirmed in this place, by your Freudian slip about letter sex. (You're right—someone should've boxed Freud's ears, strapped him to his couch and left him there.) I mean, I completely—more than anyone else in Hell—understand the appeal of bias-cut dresses and peach angora. But I find it a little weird for a straight guy to have owned those things. I mean, I get it from an Ed Wood perspective, like I said, but I've just never actually met any angora-wearing men who aren't gay, or actors. Then again, if your mother had a fondness for dressing you up in frilly things, maybe your fondness for feminine couture makes a little more sense. In a weird way. But I'm not much of a psychologist. I would've thought you'd want to get as far away from angora and satin as possible, given what I saw in my mirror. I've heard Hemingway was raised as a girl, part of the time, anyway. Hmmm . . . Maybe I've got that wrong. Didn't seem to hurt his brilliance, if it's true. Of course, he decided to make the ultimate masculine statement with a shotgun, but who am I to judge? Perhaps he was just following orders.

Did you ever learn any more about your sister?

I'm not angry that you lied about being a banker. I know firsthand that old instincts live on in this place, in defiance of logic. The truth, to my mind, is a blank canvas to which we continually add colour. (I really liked your mother's painting, by the way. She's very talented.) I don't care whether you were a banker, a file clerk or a circus clown. What does it matter now? I'm grateful you're here. (If a score is being kept, then my gratitude will probably be held against me. I should desire only that you be set free—I am too human.) I have to say it: I wish more than anything that we could meet, in the flesh, not just through a mirror. I know we both wish it. Retarded, I suppose, to be sitting in Hell dreaming of anything in the flesh. I hung up that hat, all right! Sorry, bad pun. Shut up, Velvet. Since the dream of seeing you will come to nothing, I won't bring it up again.

Your home sounds so cozy! Yellow is such a warming colour. I didn't have yellow walls at my place (I had red), but I once tried to capture what I imagine to be the mood-enhancing effect of yellow walls using a sun lamp. Obviously, it didn't work.

I'm so impressed by your taste in art. "Bouquet with Flying Lovers" is one of my very favourite Chagalls. I had a de Lempicka—"The Two Friends"—in my living room. Captures the flavor of Art Deco and yet transcends it, don't you think? I really was a bit of an art junkie—I love colour, and bare walls make me feel lonely. They remind me of hospitals. Plus, you can always pretend to yourself that your posters are originals, and feel rich. My hovel was crammed with art: Van Dongen's "Portrait of Lili Damita, the

Actress," de Chirico's "Song of Love," Kahlo's "Self-portrait with Cropped Hair" and Man Ray's "Le Violon d'Ingres." In a corner of my kitchen were stacked another de Lempicka and Van Gogh's "Starry Night" and "Café at Night," waiting to be hung. I suppose you're wondering where Edvard Munch's "The Scream" was? In the bedroom, of course! Perhaps waking up to that every morning was what finally drove me over. I just love Munch so much. "The Dance of Life" is another terrifying and beautiful favourite—I used to look it up in my art book and stare at the woman in black, the one who understands the fatality of love, for hours.

I must confess I've never cared for Degas, although I love the ballet. Too fussy. Isn't that an odd thing, considering I collected marabou feather boas?

Aside from "The Scream," there wasn't any art in my bedroom, just movie posters for *Breakfast at Tiffany's*, *Casablanca* and *A Clockwork Orange*. I would have to say that I'm more in love with silent movie stars than with their actual movies. Given the choice, I would rather hear people talk while making faces, rather than just make faces. I've always been in love with their looks, though. When I was ten, I dressed as Greta Garbo for Halloween. Nobody got it. Maybe I should've gone as a bag lady instead. (Considering Greta looked like a bag lady in her mature years, I could've still pretended to be her in my mind, but everyone else would have interpreted the costume literally.) Dressing up was a great passion of mine. I haunted thrift stores most Saturdays, looking for treasures. Believe me, I can find a sartorial diamond in the ruff (ha ha), so to speak! This skill ended up coming in very handy when Davie got me involved with the theatre company he started. He's the guy you saw in the mirror. And no, he wasn't my paramour, as you put it. More like . . . I don't know. Our relationship was a bit of a Rubik's Cube. I always sucked at Rubik's Cube. Maybe we would've been lovers if things had been different. If he had been different. Or if I had been different. If he hadn't liked boys so much. But then there were girls, too. Basically, he screwed everyone but me, except for the time . . . I don't want to talk about this anymore. I loved him. Which was stupid, I guess. He always was a bit of an asshole. But he understood me. So I loved him. And loving someone is like having a meat grinder installed in your chest. Hamburger Helper, anyone?

So sorry you saw the scene in Davie's bathroom. What else can I offer you, but an existential shrug of the shoulders and a rueful smile? It was an accident, sort of. I didn't want to . . . There was (is) a man that stalked me. I call him the Shadowman. My torturer. He was out to get me. He didn't seem to bother other people. Sometimes he would tell me to do things, and I would end up in the hospital. The doctors gave me meds and sometimes he would stay away for a while. But the meds made me feel sick and tired, and the Shadowman always came back. I hope you don't see any more of that kind of thing. No life is PG-13.

Anyway, Davie asked me to be his costume designer. A few months before I killed myself, we staged a production at Havana on Commercial Drive, which is a restaurant-cum-theatre space with a gritty, textured kind of charm. In fact, it's a happy place, a little haven, and I knew it belonged to me the day Davie took me there for lunch to discuss costumes. In the middle of the conversation, I glanced up from my spinach and artichoke salad and over to the wall, and plain to see, like a sign from the seat of the cosmos, were the words "Retro Velvet." My name was on the wall! In the midst of swirls of graffiti, proclamations of love, etc, there I was! Retro Velvet!

I had to dress all eight people in the cast on no budget, which I must say was a pleasing challenge. But Value Village came through for me in spectacular form and everyone looked fabulous. One of my greatest finds was a white satin Jean Harlow-style gown that was worn by the villainess. (The play was a detective story set in the 1920s.) Actually, come to think of it, the dress looked a lot like the one your mother was wearing. Davie played the hero's sidekick. He's such a good actor, and his impressions are legendary. You should see his Groucho Marx.

There was something so beautiful about sitting in the back of the theatre and watching lives—outfitted by me—being lived on a grand scale. I like feeling myself breathe in the dark, feeling the hush in the theatre like a blanket and seeing dust motes stream in the spotlights while people glitter. There's not enough glittering in the world at all. All we want is magic, right?

I believe now that play prolonged my life. Whether that was a good thing or a bad thing I suppose could be the subject of endless debate. The inevitable happened—does it matter if it came earlier or later? But I'll say that there was something about doing it, about existing in that rarified bubble, that temporarily gave me peace. (The Shadowman loved the play, and he gave me lots of great costume ideas. He actually complimented some of my work—his good mood was so refreshing.) Like when we watch movies, and for the time that it plays the lives onscreen supersede our own. This was like that only more so, because I helped make it—I was inside the world. Art grants temporary amnesia. I sat at the back of the theatre and saw only other people's tears and tantrums, joys and heartbreaks, faces and costumes. Did you ever feel as though you were outside of yourself, watching? I felt like that always, except for those nights in the last row. Even when the Shadowman came to visit, a part of me was standing back, watching it happen. But in the back row of the theatre I wasn't watching myself, I was only conscious of this other world before me.

Except for that time, I've never been able to shake the sensation of floating, as though I've come untethered and I'm drifting somewhere up above my head, always looking down, scrutinizing, watching my every move. Were there ever moments, looking at yourself in the mirror (I know you don't like mirrors, but I also know there were times you looked) when you didn't recognize what you saw? I sometimes stood in front of a mirror for hours, searching for something—I'm not sure what. Pulling on my hair to watch my face change, testing to see if I was real. Touching my fingers to the glass and expecting them to pass right through, as if into water, because everything seemed like an illusion. The woman in the mirror was always a stranger. I have been accused of being vain (by Davie and my mother), a person who catches glimpses of herself in store windows, hand to her hair, pursing her lips, but I was only testing to see where the edges of me were, where I began and ended, whether or not my ball-and-chain body was still around.

Whenever I picked up a pen, the girl that was floating up above my head would suddenly anchor. Well no, that's not true. For the most part, that last statement would fall into Life's Column of Bullshit Wishful Thinking. But in the best moments, she would anchor and be still, and in that stillness the mast of a story would unfurl, no illusions, no folding mirrors, no pain. Sometimes—no Shadowman. Or even better, he would stand there—in a good mood—and throw out the most fabulous ideas. I was writing a novella about a company of interstellar circus performers—always been a deep admirer of people who can juggle flaming torches. I wanted the Shadowman to be a character in the book, but he wouldn't let me, of course. He accused me of trying to use him for publicity. I wasn't just a waitress in a Thai café, or a onetime costume designer for a shoestring theatre troupe! I started writing stories when I was six—my smash debut was entitled "Mr. Aardvark Ties His Shoes." I hope I'm accurate when I say I've progressed since then. I actually had a couple of stories published in high school, in small fringe journals that pay you with a copy of the magazine. I did a lot of writing at school in the bathroom stall farthest from the door, under a pebbled glass window, at lunchtime. There's something deliciously subversive about doing creative work that no one knows about in a place where you would never be suspected. Also, there's no revenge like painting a cruel picture of someone you hate with words.

I've since had quite a few stories published in lit journals, mostly tiny publications run out of a garret, so to speak. I considered those small victories to be target practice. Wrote poems too, but I never showed them to anyone. Sometimes the Shadowman would dictate his poetic inspirations to me and I would be forced to write his verses for him. I hated doing that. He has a fondness for violent imagery. (Maybe you think I'm crazy because I see things that other people don't see. But Davie always said it made me interesting. And lonely.) I'd been working on my novella for about a year, but it was a nerve-destroying, hair-pulling process. Many nights I spent studying my red walls, tapping at them with my index finger as though I expected a "Mouth of Truth," just like the one in *Roman Holiday*, to appear and spew forth the key to genius, or lying on the couch counting the bumps on the ceiling, as if some final number might be the mathematical proof I needed to solve the question of why it was so hard to create. I guess part of why it was so hard was the Shadowman. He'd come up with great ideas, but sometimes he'd suddenly insist I cross out what I'd written. I always felt as though I was writing (and living) against a tide, and in the last months, that tide was washing out my will.

Maybe I should've written a script instead—a movie for Davie to star in. Not that he deserved it. But what people get and what they deserve seem to be random factors in life. Are we meat puppets playing out a script? The whim of a sadistic playwright's hand?

I had a father, but he died in an accident before I was born. Actually, he was run over by a car, same as you. So I spent much of my life missing him even though I'd never met him, wondering where he was and what he was doing, until I trained myself not to think about it. Now I'm wondering about him again. I suppose I half expected him to knock on the door, say "Hi Velvet, nice to meet you" and provide some further instructions. But I don't think that's going to happen. I guess he went to Heaven.

I'll shut up now.

Sincerely, Velvet

7

I lay on my back doing Pilates exercises because I have always found if you do something physical you don't have to think as much, not because I cared about having tight abs in Hell. I kept my eyes on the frozen 8:57 clock.

When my stomach hurt as much as I could stand, I collapsed flat out, closing my eyes so I wouldn't be tempted to count the bumps on the ceiling. How long had I been in here? No wrinkles yet—in fact, I seemed to look younger. Having spun off the treadmill of tick tock, I couldn't even take a guess. Back on planet Earth, time seemed an incontestable reality: measured, estimated, swallowed up, drawn out. But in the pink room with the broken clock and the window that looked out on a meta-landscape of white, time was a flimsy nothing. From the moment the heavy door shut behind me, or no, wait; from the moment I went whizzing down the slide in the dark, the ticker-tape continuum bent, and life in a bedroom bubble began.

And it was a good thing I didn't feel hungry, since room service had not appeared at the door. Nor did I have to pee, a fact I also counted as a major blessing. When I thought about food, the coconut curries I ate every workday, or the three bars of bittersweet chocolate I went through once a month, it was with a sensation of fond nostalgia and sharp sadness, but it did not evoke any physical longing in me.

It was people I longed for.

INT. BRINKLEY'S HELL–MIRROR–
VELVET'S CHILDHOOD HOME–BEDROOM–NIGHT

Mae/Mother bursts through Velvet's bedroom door, book in hand, wearing a glittering black cape. The remains of a black eye still mar her face.

MAE/MOTHER

Gather 'round, child! It's story hour!

VELVET

(solemnly)

Children.

MAE/MOTHER

Huh?

VELVET

Children. There are two of us.

MAE/MOTHER

Hmmm . . . that's interesting. I only see one. So either I'm blind, there's a kid under the bed, or you're crazy. Which is it?

VELVET

I guess you're blind. She's sitting right beside me.

MAE/MOTHER

Velvet, we talked about this. I thought you got rid of your imaginary friend.

VELVET

She's not imaginary. And I did, but she came back. She missed me.

MAE/MOTHER

You're givin' me the creeps. I wasn't prepared to read for an audience of more than one.

VELVET

She would prefer you refer to her by name.

MAE/MOTHER

She has a name?

VELVET

Delilah.

MAE/MOTHER

Delilah? Jesus. You're not gettin' biblical on me, are you?

VELVET

That's her name. She wants to know if you're going to read the story about the pigs.

MAE/MOTHER

No, I'm going to read the story about the witches. That's why I wore the cape. You know I can't do my "Bubble, bubble, toil and trouble" routine without a costume. Oh, wait a second. I left my martini in the bathroom.

Mae/Mother exits, cape flying, and Velvet pulls the covers up to her chin.

VELVET

(to Delilah)

I'm cold. Are you? You'll like this one. Mom's a great story-reader. Just make sure to be quiet. She doesn't like to be interrupted while she's performing.

The cape-clad woman flies back in, sloshing some of her martini on the carpet.

MAE/MOTHER

Fuck. Oh well. These carpets need disinfecting any-way.

She takes a big drink, wipes her mouth and places the glass on the dresser.

MAE/MOTHER

(clears throat)

Now.

VELVET

Delilah is very much looking forward to the performance.

MAE/MOTHER

For fuck's sake, Velvet, can't you get some real friends? Isn't there anyone in your class you like?

VELVET

(with great dignity)

No.

Mae/Mother flings herself to the floor.

MAE/MOTHER

You'll be the death of me! You're killing me, you're killing me, I'm dying, I'm dying, I'm dead!

A long silence, during which Velvet peers over the bed at her mother's prone form. Then the dead woman pops to her feet.

MAE/MOTHER

Fine, be a freak. But I don't recommend going around telling the kids at school about your little friend. Speaking of freaks, how's my eye? Can you notice it much?

VELVET

Yeah.

The witchy drama queen pouts, touches the bruise.

MAE/MOTHER

You coulda lied. Think it'll be better by Saturday? I got a date. Think I can cover it with make-up? I've done that before, but it usually still shows through a bit.

VELVET

Maybe you should cancel.

MAE/MOTHER

Uh-uh. This one's different.

VELVET

You always look pretty to me.

Mae/Mother drops the storybook to the floor and starts to cry. She climbs onto the bed and wraps Velvet in her arms and cape.

MAE/MOTHER

My little angel, my little angel. Mommy loves you so much! Don't forget. Don't ever forget.

(wipes her tears and sniffles)

Oh Vee, you get tits and life goes to rat shit.

VELVET

I don't want tits.

MAE/MOTHER

They come in handy sometimes.

VELVET

Delilah doesn't want tits either.

MAE/MOTHER

Does she want a story?

VELVET

(nodding)

So do I.

Mae/Mother leaps off the bed, retrieves the storybook from the floor and spreads her arms wide.

MAE/MOTHER

Very well. In honour of my daughter Velvet and her invisible friend Delilah, I will now present to you *The Witching Hour*, by Cedric Culpepper. Lights, please.

Velvet turns on her bedside lamp. Mae/Mother turns off the overhead light.

MAE/MOTHER

There.

(clears throat)

Now, by the light of a huntress moon and a sixty-watt bulb, I will regale you with tales from the dark side.

(in a low, slow, chilling voice)

"Once upon a time, in the very dead of night . . ."

8

Dear Velvet,

My mother was not crazy, I will have you know. I would expect that someone who was sensitive enough to the vagaries of life that she killed herself—and had an ongoing, emotionally charged dalliance with a Shadowman—would be rather less blunt in speaking about a person's mother. Granted, she was troubled. Very sensitive, a painter. But I dislike the word "crazy." An abominable word. Careful, Velvet, not to dole out labels and judgments here. Doing so will not help your case, if there is a case to be made. Those begging for mercy should be choosier about the words they use.

She needed me. Always. And so I stayed with her. Because I am a nice person. She missed her little girl, as you saw. My sister. I guess I wasn't a very good substitute. Which makes me sad. Her little girl went missing from a grocery store two years before I was born. Gone forever.

Your mother could be described as troubled as well, from what I have seen. But I agree with your childhood assessment. She's a great story-reader.

Everything I know about feminine dress I learned from my mother. I hated wearing dresses when I was a little boy. But for some reason, I like it now. I don't know why.

I should not have told you about the dresses, or the peach angora. (But since you already saw me in your mirror as a little boy wearing a dress, it stands to reason that you may see me as a grown man, also wearing a dress.) You could not possibly understand. I am not sure why I did tell you so readily, why I was so very eager to be honest about my occasional style of dress, and not about other things. It seems that a fluorescently-lit bedroom cell in Hell brings out one's confessional spirit only on an intermittent basis. I am not gay. (As Clara Bow could attest.) I am not a drag queen. I am a man with a taste for fine fabrics. As a result, I sometimes wore dresses. Not on the street, just in my bedroom. Clara understood. She loved clothes. As you well know, there is nothing like the feel of a flowing dress swishing against your skin. My comprehension of this puts me in the upper echelon of sensual creatures.

Somehow, I was not at all surprised to learn that you are a writer. Please tell me more about the novella you were writing. Speaking of writing (or writing of writing, rather), the "screenwriter" responsible for our earthly debacles must have a vicious streak. Though aside from being run over by a car, I suppose I cannot really complain about my life. Relatively uneventful, as it was. But from this vantage point, I suppose it is an interesting prospect to see one's time on Earth in filmic terms. A sad movie, a shot of bleak Gallic cinema! There is no joy in acting such a play. Though perhaps we are trapped in a clip of Gallic cinema right now! Better to fancy our lives had more of a Latin filmic flavor, or, in ancient terms, minor Greek tragedy (no offense to Homer). What am I saying? Who wants to watch one's life onscreen? Living the scenes was enough—I do not desire a catalogue. Even cinephiles have their limit.

I was a bibliophile, too. In my life on the spinning rock, I loved to read anything and everything. I had checked out most of the books in the library, until I stopped because the pages were filthy and stuck together, and apparently a lot of people who take books out of the library do not have great hand-eye coordination when it comes to drinking coffee while reading. I became a book buyer instead. Sometimes I just stared at the names in the phone book if I did not have more interesting reading material in the house. *Dogs in North America Annual* was my favourite magazine. (Of course, I did not really want to own a dog, given the inherent cleanliness issues, but I liked looking at them.) I confess to a weakness for the Bichon Frisé. Not because I have a desire to style their hair or anything like that. Their faces remind me of Christmas.

While we are on the topic of writing (well, sort of—I am veering back in that direction) I will confess something else: I had started a book of my own. Are you familiar with Harlequin romance novels? I like a story with a happy ending. On a whim I picked one up in a drugstore one day and I was hooked. They let anybody take a stab at writing one, you know. There is a formula that is really quite mathematical in its precision. They send it to you and you invent the rest. I thought, how hard could this be? And they pay you for it.

So I started writing like mad. In my most recent attempt, the heroine's name was Eleanor, and the hero's name was Declan. I was about a quarter of the way in when I was run over. It starts out with Eleanor, a young grieving widow American expatriate, running a bed-and-breakfast out of a medieval manor in the Cotswolds. Declan is a figure surrounded by mystery. He comes to stay with her, but he carries secrets that, unbeknownst to her, connect him to her past. I was still unsure what those secrets were, but that was the general idea of the book. It was dedicated to my favourite movie star, Clara Bow.

INT. VELVET'S HELL—MIRROR—
BRINKLEY'S BEDROOM—NIGHT

Brinkley sits at his little wooden desk, pen in hand, notebook open before him, clad in a white satin bias-cut dress and a peach angora cardigan. The 1920s film star Clara Bow stares from a large black-and-white glossy photograph pasted to a mirror that hangs on the wall. Impish, knowing sexuality quartzes out of her kohl-heavy eyes. Brinkley sighs and grinds his knuckles into his eye sockets. He begins to cross out what he has written in his book, gathering momentum as he slashes his pen back and forth across the page. The paper rips and he throws his pen against the wall and tears at his notebook. His eyes are red and damp. He crumples several pages and disposes of them in a wastebasket beside his desk. Sniffling, he pulls Kleenex from a dispenser, a Cotswold-style cottage that emits Kleenex from its chimney, and turns to Clara Bow in the mirror.

BRINKLEY

Please tell me how to proceed, Clara. Perhaps a Harlequin romance is beyond me. My description of the Cotswold scenery is perfect, I think. But I seem to be lacking any, shall I say, erotica, which poses a problem when one is writing a romance novel.

The photograph of Clara Bow comes to life.

CLARA BOW

(strong Brooklyn accent)

I ain't no writer, honey. But this I know fer sure. Ain't nobody gonna read a romance novel that only has descriptions uh trees in it.

(shrugs)

Nothin' romantic 'bout greenery, darlin'.

BRINKLEY

You are right, completely right. But I seem unable to fix the problem. I am no Marlowe. Now *he* was a romantic.

CLARA BOW

I got no idea who this Marlowe character is, but you gotta put feelin' into it. That's what people want. Like me. I can cry on cue, ya know. Watch this.

In an instant tears cascade from Clara's eyes, silky streaks of slipperiness highlighting the apple contours of her cheeks. The baffled, pure pain of a wounded animal swirls in the dark fathoms of her gaze. In response, Brinkley's eyes well and tears fall in profusion down his face.

BRINKLEY

Please don't cry. I hate it when you cry. It makes me cry.

(buries his face in his hands)

Oh, I can't look.

His shoulders begin to shake.

CLARA BOW

Brinkley, hey Brinkley!

He looks up.

CLARA BOW

Hey silly! What are ya gonna cry for? I'm just puttin' on a show. Directors are amazed that I can do that. But I gotta park my chewing gum behind my ear. I don't like ta cry when I got gum in my mouth.

BRINKLEY

But you look so sad.

CLARA BOW

Well yeah. I gotta lotta sad things I can think about. Makes me cry inna second. The fans love me, ya know.

BRINKLEY

Of course they do. You are the "It Girl" of the '20s. But nobody loves you as much as me. I love you dearly, Clara. So please don't cry anymore. The only time I ever cry is when I talk to you.

CLARA BOW

Then ya should talkta me more often. Cryin's good for the soul. If ya can scream at the same time, even bettah. There's nothin' so refreshin' as throwin' yaself on the floor and screamin' bloody murder. My ma used ta have fits.

BRINKLEY

Really?

CLARA BOW

Well not a real fit, more like a spell. But not a regular faintin' spell neither, somethin' else. She couldn't breathe. I don't have spells. I'm just an insomniac.

BRINKLEY

I will stay awake with you. My mother can't sleep either. So she takes pills. Her moaning keeps me awake. I can't stand it.

(pause)

Will you help me with my book?

CLARA BOW

You're as good as gold, sweetheart, as good as fuckin' gold. Yer ma don't deserve a precious son like you. Yer book, you say? Like I said, I'm no writer, but I think I gotta line for ya.

BRINKLEY

You do? What is it?

CLARA BOW

"He scooped her up in his arms, carried her to the bed, and there on the satin sheets they were carried away by wings of desire."

Brinkley jumps out of his chair.

BRINKLEY

Let me find my pen! I need to write this down!

He retrieves his pen and rushes back to the desk, scribbles Clara's line.

CLARA BOW

Ya got it? Get it? *Wings*! That's uh movie uh mine!

BRINKLEY

I love that film! I love all your films.

CLARA BOW

That's a nice dress ya got on, by the way. I used ta have one just like it.

BRINKLEY

It's one of my mother's old ones. It's so smooth.

CLARA BOW

I'm so fuckin' tired, Brinkley. But I can't sleep. I can't ever sleep. Will you sing to me? Nobody ever sings me a lullaby.

BRINKLEY

I can't sing at all. I'm no vocalist by any stretch of the imagination. I'm a tad short on rhythm and my ability to harmonize is compromised by—

CLARA BOW

Please. Sing or I'll cry.

BRINKLEY

No! Please don't cry! I'll sing. Umm . . . I am not sure I know any lullabies.

CLARA BOW

(threatening)

I'm gonna cry . . .

BRINKLEY

Gee whiz, Clara. Jesus Murphy. You're so hard on me.

CLARA BOW

Are you using the Lord's name in vain?

BRINKLEY

No. The Lord's name isn't Murphy. I don't think.

CLARA BOW

I hope not. Murphy's a dog's name.

BRINKLEY

Since when are you religious?

CLARA BOW

Sing dammit! I can feel the tears comin'!

BRINKLEY

Wait! I know a Welsh lullaby that my mother used to sing to me. She has Welsh and Irish roots. That's why she has red hair. She's a beautiful Irish colleen.

CLARA BOW

(threatening)

Is she as beautiful as me?

BRINKLEY

No! Never as beautiful as you.

CLARA BOW

So sing it.

Brinkley stands and clasps his hands, clears his throat.

BRINKLEY

"Sleep my love and peace attend thee
All through the night . . .
Guardian angels God will lend thee
All through the night . . ."

I really liked the challenge of creating within set boundaries, like the way I imagine great sonnet writers loved the thrill of contorting words to fit. Not that I am comparing myself to any great sonnet writers, mind you. Now that you have brought up writing I am thinking about my characters again. I used to lie awake at night, much like you described—except I did not tap on my walls—and play out scenes in my head. Like your Shadowman, Clara would sometimes give me the occasional line, or good idea. But she's an actress, not a writer. From what I had read of Harlequin romance novels, there is quite a license to be dramatic. I bet you have a real talent for writing that sort of thing. I wonder if I would have made money at it.

Prior to the English countryside plot I had tried three others. One was set in a small Minnesota town, one in Paris and the other in Tuscany. I have never travelled to any of those places, just like I have not travelled to the Cotswolds, but I bought guidebooks and thought that I could improvise my way. But nothing in the first three really seemed to jell. I am not sure why. I think it is important to select the right names for your characters; if you name them wrongly they simply refuse to animate. Maybe that is what happened. I was on the wrong nomenclatural path. I did hit on the perfect nom de plume for myself, though. I am not sure if anyone writes Harlequin romance novels under their real name, which is kind of a shame. And a man's name is, of course, not really appropriate. So: "Charlotte O'Shaughnessy." It has a nice ring to it, does it not? I was a reverse George Eliot!

I cannot believe we share such similar taste in art—and movies. I watched *Casablanca* 611 times. That may seem like a lot, but you really do notice something different with each viewing. It is my favourite movie, aside from the ones starring Clara Bow. No star was ever as beautiful. She had a very tragic life. Sometimes, in her films, her eyes are so bottomless with sorrow it is as if she is appealing directly to the audience for rescue and salvation. But I digress . . . I tried to watch *A Clockwork Orange* once, but I only made it to the halfway mark. It gave me nightmares.

I can picture you as a costume designer! I have always been an admirer of people in the theatre. I went to a few plays in Toronto, and you are quite right, there was magic in the air. Except for a really bad production of *Picnic*. The leading actress sounded like she had sucked helium backstage, and the leading man was about twenty years too old for the part. Anyway, while seeing a good play you do forget everything else. I was more of a watch-movies-at-home-guy, though, especially in the last year before I died. All of those people gathered in one theatre at one time I found a bit unnerving, and while I know not everyone thinks this way, I was growing more bothered at the thought of who might have sat in my seat before me. Again, the germ predicament. I know you understand.

I was very interested in the floating sensation you described. I am not sure I have ever experienced that. Sometimes, just as I was falling asleep, I experienced a floating-spinning sensation, as though I was commencing warp speed to another planet. But then I might have been, and simply failed in my takeoff. You know, astral projection. Perhaps to Andromeda, where I might have originated. Was your novella set in Andromeda? You mentioned interstellar circus performers—fascinating stuff. In everyday life—on Earth—I had more of a trembly feeling, the sense that my heart was beating too loud and everyone could hear. I guess you had the "floats" and I had the "shakes." Maybe shaking and floating are two forms of the same thing.

In light of our respective mirror revelations, is it possible to believe that reality is in fact a film, stored away in a Great Canister somewhere? Are we real? Or are we scraps on the editing room floor? And if we have been cut from the story, does that mean we do not exist at all? How would we know? We are in an interesting position to debate this. We are still real, are we not? I feel that I am. Perhaps that is the key: I feel.

I have two degrees: a Bachelor of Arts and a Bachelor of Science. You see, I could not quite make up my mind. I am a bit of a dabbler, a bit of a dilettante. So I drifted here, I drifted there, but in the end I am not sure what it all amounted to.

I know what it is like to miss a father that you do not remember. It taxes one's powers of invention.

I do not think my mother loves me, anymore. Actually, sometimes I questioned whether she ever did. If she did, she doesn't now. But that is a different story.

Velvet, my eyes are now as blue as the ocean. When the scenes in my mirror stop playing, the electronic snow only remains for a while, and then the mirror once again becomes a faithful reflector of my room and me. Right now it shows that my eyes are lit with a strange light, an alien glow. Maybe these are my original eyes. How about yours?

How long do you think we have been here? In some moments it feels like forever, and in others only a few minutes. I am afraid I cannot even hazard a guess. I suppose it is irrelevant. Do you have this same sensation? The sensation that your ability to judge time has gone from you, that you exist in a Black Hole? I imagine you do. And I guess that we do exist in a Black Hole, in actual fact—it is not merely a sensation. I once read that the time continuum is like a piece of twisted ribbon, and if we knew enough we could slide back and forth along it. We could also walk through walls. But that is a different story.

I would like to learn more about the Shadowman. Could it be possible that you and I are alike? I've never met anyone like me before. Loneliness is a disease that is hard to cure, is it not?

I am not hungry, which is a great blessing. I hope you are not hungry. Perhaps we will not be tortured on all fronts.

Have you ever heard such quiet in your life?

Yours very truly,

Brinkley

Jesus. Someone's a little sensitive about his mother. How dare he lecture me about sensitivity, or my fate—if I still had one. Sanctimonious little shit. (I had written "Dear Brinkley, Fuck you" at the top of a page, but then decided that if I did indeed have a case to plead, writing such a letter would not be a point for the defence. *The Devil made me do it!* I could probably plead that I didn't know the rules of social etiquette still applied in Hell. I thought honesty and bluntness were requirements in the pursuit of "Truth." Were we pursuing "Truth"? What for? Well, we had nothing better to do. When in doubt, a little existentialist philosophizing never hurt anyone.) Seriously, if you can't tell it like it is to your next-door neighbour in Hell, who *can* you be honest with? So he thinks "crazy" is an abominable word. (And speaking of abominable words, who uses a word like "abominable?") This from a man who I'd just watched carry on a conversation with—and sing a lullaby to—a long-dead movie star. (So Clara Bow was some sort of time traveller? Or Brinkley needed a pharmaceutical adjustment? And why was she so interested in him, anyway?) And Harlequin romance novels? A *guy* who writes Harlequin romance novels? Of course, it's not that he was claiming to be composing any great masterpiece, and I have always maintained a love for the "beauty school dropouts of life," so to speak, but . . . A reverse George Eliot? Well, there was, I had to admit, something faintly daring about a man writing a romance novel. And why did he think I would be great at writing that kind of stuff? Was that supposed to be a compliment? (I hoped he wasn't expecting me to become his romance-writing-partner. Hell's Harlequin duo. The Ellery Queen of bodice-rippers.) Anyway, he'd seen me carve up my wrist in Davie's bathroom. I could use the word "crazy" if I wanted to. (I was terrified about what else the mirror might show him. Funny, the desire to keep up appearances never goes away. Well, he knew about the Shadowman. It was a little late for image maintenance. But I had not been, as he so wrongly put it, having a dalliance with the Shadowman—he was a stalker, not a lover.) And yes, he was right, my mother was bonks, too. So what? We're all a bunch of crazies. You can love someone and still call a spade a spade.

The scene of Brinkley (one who apparently took celebrity worship a bit too far) in my mirror, and the electronic snow that followed it, had vanished. I approached the glass; my eyes were blue. Not blue running helter-skelter over blackish, but pure brilliant aquamarine. They were glowing and free of bruising or blood vessels; they were larger than I remembered and so limpid as to be almost watery, like you could touch them and rings would shudder out to the edges. Everything else looked the same except my eyebrows, which, upon close-up inspection an inch from the glass, appeared to be finer and fairer, with several very blonde hairs that looked white amidst the darker ones. I attempted to take deep breaths, but my diaphragm failed me, and they turned into short, shallow gasps that quickened until I leaned into the wall, saw silver stars, and then sank to the floor. I lay on my back with my head turned to one side, looking into the dim under the bed.

I went through a phase once where I wore coloured contact lenses all the time: blue, green, purple, hazel, amber. I thought blackish-brown eyes were boring, and I liked being able to match my irises to my outfits. In fact, I often wished that eyes were like one of those slot machines with the pictures that you try to match up; I wanted to pull a lever on the side of my head and have my eyeballs spin to a different hue. Though looking back, if I'm forced to admit it, there was something comforting about being able to take out my eye colour at night and see the same old eyes staring back at me. Contacts were part of my costume, part of the armour. This was different. My eyes, like Brinkley's, looked alien. Speaking of alien, he originated in Andromeda? Oh my God! Who's really the nuttiest person in Hell? And why, despite the fact that he was a sanctimonious little shit, did his bizarreness make him so appealing? Typical, Velvet, you always go for the loons, and even in Hotel Hades you're no different. Of course, to be fair—and when one is being held captive by self-evaluation, I guess fairness is somewhat inevitable—I didn't really have the right to call him crazy, without being sanctimonious myself. The Shadowman had always seemed to be my one big problem—a huge problem, I admit—but I considered myself pretty normal, otherwise. Brinkley appeared to have so many oddities. But so what? It was kind of comforting, seeing his weirdness. And him seeing mine. It's funny, even in Hell, the urge to consider oneself better than another is ever-present. Anyway, there was something otherworldly about my irises' H2O-glow, no sign of my personality or memories dog-paddling the blue depths, only an infant's purity. I was sporting the Tabula Rasa of eyeballs.

Unidentified scary-movie-music thrummed through my head. In my mind's eye I was dressed in a trench coat, drawing a pistol from my pocket as I moved toward a blind corner. A mist floated across my imaginary moon and footsteps tickled the air. I drew my lids shut and tried to feel if there was any change in sensation beneath them: heat or cold, pain. Everything felt the same. And I could still see. So far.

It was comforting to know that Brinkley's eyes were in the same boat. (If I'm going down, man, you're coming with me.) Both of us, apparently, without a lifejacket.

He said his "blue as the ocean" eyes were the only change that he had noted on himself thus far. Another live wire of fear sparked through me. I ran my fingers over my eyebrows, usually so dense and dark. Was my hair next?

I wondered where the Shadowman was. He hadn't shown up in a while, which was odd, especially since I had stopped taking my meds three or four months before I'd hung myself, and my little corner of Hell had already failed to protect me from his onslaught. But I felt quite lucid, clear like my eyes. Had Hell decided to save me from the Hell of the Shadowman? Doubtful. (Wishful thinking is like crack cocaine—one hit and you're hooked.)

I looked over Brinkley's letter yet again. After his initial snit, his tone seemed warm and confiding. Hmmm . . . moody. Something about his crazy mother bothered me. And it obviously bothered him, too. *I do not think my mother loves me, anymore.*

Anymore?

Dear Brinkley,

For one so sensitive about his mother, you don't seem to be sensitive about much else. (And while we're being insensitive, how about this: You look terrible in women's clothes, and the fact that you wore your mother's old dresses is sick. Sure, Ed Wood was a cross-dresser, but he didn't wear his own mother's dresses!) Yes, I used my favourite retro belt to hang myself in my bathroom, but you don't have the right to touch that, ever. (And ever, as we are discovering, is a very long time.) Not in a fashion that's meant to hurt me, anyway. If I can't be honest with you about what I see in my mirror, then what's the point of writing to each other at all? Your mother was clearly a nutter, although beautiful and, I'm sure, sensitive (in a twisted sort of way) at the same time. (Why don't you think she loves you anymore? Surely she doesn't blame you for being hit by a car. What aren't you telling me?) Your mother had every right to be nuts, given she'd forever lost her daughter while grocery shopping. What a horrible burden to carry. Or maybe she was troubled before that. At any rate, it makes sense to me why she wanted to dress you like a girl. Sucked to be you, though.

And yes, my mother certainly had her moments, too. And having been a special guest at the Cracker Farm more than once, and then having done what I did, I'm sure that people would say that my brain is a bit of a doily. So what? Craziness is a country with closely guarded borders: you got to be special to get in and, once you're a resident, they don't ever let you out. You should know that, Mr. Crazy-Is-An-Abominable-Word. I saw you. You and Clara. A rather long time you spent talking to a dead movie star. And singing a lullaby to her. (Which I thought, incidentally, was one of the most beautiful things I've ever heard. The Welsh really know how to write bedtime songs.) So I guess I'm inside your head now. And you're inside mine. Great. I already had enough weird stuff going on upstairs.

Oh, and the Andromeda thing. How wacked out is that? But I love it! (Do you think I could be from Andromeda, too? Are Deco-loving creative types popular there? Do Andromedans go in for human sacrifice? Chopping off someone's existence in the name of the gods has always seemed to make people feel better. Really, I'm surprised we haven't kept it up on our patch of the world's grass, lobbed a few young virgins off the parliament buildings. And no, my novella wasn't set in Andromeda. Yes, I was writing about interstellar circus performers, but I was creating my own galaxy for them. Actually, that was the Shadowman's idea. As much as I hate him, I have to give him credit for all of his interesting creative inspirations.) My best friend when I was a kid, Delilah, used to tell me she was from Venus. Who knows, you two might've met on an intergalactic trip. I'm open-minded.

My eyes are blue, just like yours. They look alien to me and not just because of the colour. They have taken on a watery sort of glow, and the bruising around one eye caused by throwing myself against the wall has disappeared. There are no blood vessels either, only pure white and pure blue. They look larger than I remember—two large liquid jewels. Once upon a time I might have thought this a good thing, but not now. I'm afraid to look in the mirror, for fear of what I might discover next. But I'm longing for more movies of you. I want to understand your life. I have something else to announce as well: my eyebrows appear to be lightening and growing finer. I'm panicking. What's happening to us? Well, I know you don't have the answer since you're asking me the same question. I'm wracking my brain for possibilities, but thus far to no avail. I can only surmise that my eyebrows are the opening act for a metamorphosis involving my hair. You haven't mentioned that you're in any physical pain. Neither am I, since I stopped throwing myself against the wall. And obviously you can still see, since you haven't stopped writing letters. For these mercies I'm very thankful, but Brinkley—foreboding makes it hard to breathe. I'm terrified of my own reflection. Funny, I think I felt the same way before I died. My eyes are beautiful and grotesque.

So you were writing a romance novel. Surprising. And kind of odd, for a man. From what I saw in my mirror, you were having trouble with it. Romance is hard to write. But we really do need more stories with happy endings. My novella was not going to end on a happy note and look where it got me. The Shadowman doesn't like happy endings. My main character's name was Roma. I picked that name because I was in a produce market one day when a vision of the character came into my head and I was holding a Roma tomato in my hand. It was like seeing my name on the wall of Havana Restaurant—a clear sign. She was a young trapeze artist who became entangled in an affair with a much, much older man named Victor, who was a ventriloquist with a collection of real-potato Mr. Potato Heads and an addiction to takeout Chinese food. I was creating a circus-themed alternate galaxy for them to live in, but it was hard to write when the Shadowman kept interrupting and telling me what to do. Sure, sometimes his ideas were genius, but sometimes . . . not so much. There is nothing so horrible as an unfinished would-be masterpiece gone stale.

We are real. I'm sure of that. Reality clearly has more facets than we ever thought possible. We couldn't write letters to one another if we weren't real. We couldn't cry or long for the things we once had. We are still us, even though our eyes are no longer our own. You're right: I feel, therefore I am. Are you a Pisces, by any chance?

My friend Davie used to say, in fits of existential brilliance brought on by several martinis: I fuck, therefore I am. I think that's rather crude, don't you? That was Davie, funny and crude. This place would turn Descartes on his ear.

I can't believe you watched *Casablanca* 611 times! I saw it 137 times and I thought I held the record. I know all the dialogue by heart. I can recite the film from start to finish. I once did it in front of my mirror, just to test myself. Not really a skill that came in handy. Not being able to watch *A Clockwork Orange* is a sign of a very healthy individual—the germ thing be damned!— and I'm like you; I had cinema-prompted nightmares all the time. When I was a child, I was traumatized by Michael Jackson's "Thriller" video. But a few months before the end, I decided, for no good reason that I can think of now, to try to cure myself of movie squeamishness. So I forced myself to watch *A Clockwork Orange* ten times in a row. Not only did that not cure me of my fear, I didn't sleep for a week. Thereafter, I slept with the lights on surrounded by a fortress of pillows. I hung the poster in my room partly as a nod to what I can admit is brilliant filmmaking, but mostly as a reminder to myself not to be such an idiot.

So this was my I'm-going-to-be-reasonable-and-forgiving-in-case-there-is-a-God letter, when what I really wanted to do after I read the first part of your last letter was drop you like a hot rock. Get over yourself. "Crazy" is not an abominable word. Your mother was nuts, I'm nuts, you're nuts, and who really gives a shit about semantics in Hell? Have you ever taken a trip to the Cracker Farm? They usually put people who talk to dead movie stars on medication, you know. (Unless Clara Bow really is a time traveller, but then again, even if she is, nobody would believe that.) But sometimes pills make everything worse. They made me sick and tired and dizzy. It was either that, or the Shadowman, or sometimes both—pretty shitty options, if you ask me. Also, for the record, I was not having a "dalliance" with the Shadowman. He was my torturer, not my boyfriend. Okay, so he was sort of my friend too, in a weird way, but not really. Anyhow, if you ever accuse me of being an insensitive suicide again, or make any other insensitive references to my untimely end, you will be spending Eternity alone. And that's a long time.

Sincerely, Velvet

P.S. Is your hair turning colours, yet?

9

INT. BRINKLEY'S HELL—MIRROR—
VELVET'S CHILDHOOD HOME—BEDROOM—AFTERNOON

Mae/Mother jumps naked on her bed.

MAE/MOTHER
(hollering)
Vee! Vee!

Velvet appears in the doorway.

MAE/MOTHER
Darling, help me decide what to wear. He's gonna be here in three hours. Be an angel and pour me a drink. Over there.

She points to a bottle of gin and a glass on the dresser. Velvet walks over and pours.

VELVET
I was just teaching Delilah how to write Roman numerals. She thinks they're more elegant than regular numbers.

MAE/MOTHER

Oh, for Chrissake. Well, you two'll be all set if you ever run into Julius Caesar.

VELVET

Who?

MAE/MOTHER

Never mind. Just help me pick something to wear. Men want the gift but you gotta wrap it well.

Her gifts fly in all directions as she jumps.

VELVET

Mom?

MAE/MOTHER

Yeah?

VELVET

I think I'm getting pneumonia. Delilah's got it too.

MAE/MOTHER

Why do you think that?

VELVET

Sore throat.

MAE/MOTHER

Just a little cold. I'll leave the Dimetapp bottle in your room. Take a swig before you go to sleep. And I'll make you some chicken soup and chow mein tomorrow.

VELVET

Mom?

MAE/MOTHER

Yeah?

VELVET

I don't want you to have a date.

Mae/Mother stops jumping and drops to her knees. She holds out her arms and Velvet rushes into them.

MAE/MOTHER

This one's different, baby, I promise you this one's different.

Velvet's face is torrented by tears. She shakes her head.

MAE/MOTHER

Yes, yes he is. This one's gonna be different, angel.

She wipes Velvet's face with her hands.

VELVET

Pinky swear?

MAE/MOTHER

Pinky swear. Now: what should I wear? And darling bring me that drink, chop, chop, I'm in the bloody Sahara over here.

INT. BRINKLEY'S HELL—MIRROR—
VELVET'S CHILDHOOD HOME—HALL STAIRS—LATER

Velvet sits on the stairs, a pink blanket around her shoulders. She listens to the loud conversation emanating from the kitchen.

INT. BRINKLEY'S HELL—
VELVET'S CHILDHOOD HOME—KITCHEN—CONTINUOUS

Mae/Mother stands at the counter pouring drinks, waving her arms about as she speaks. A face full of make-up diminishes, but does not entirely hide, the shadow of her black eye. Her date sits at the table, digging his gums with a toothpick.

MAE/MOTHER

(loudly)

We gotta be quiet, my daughter's asleep. Hope you didn't mind coming here. Babysitters are expensive.

TOOTHPICK MAN

(looking around)

Doesn't look like you're doing too badly for yourself.

MAE/MOTHER

Oh, it's an old house. My dad left it to me in his will. Otherwise I'd still be renting a dumpy apartment.

TOOTHPICK MAN

Thanks for dinner. You're a great cook.

MAE/MOTHER

Anytime.

She sashays to the table and hands him his drink, sits on his lap. He touches a finger to the bruise on her face.

TOOTHPICK MAN

You gotta be more careful, honey.

MAE/MOTHER

(turning her face away)

Yeah, I know. I'm a fucking klutz. That's what happens when doors jump out at you.

Toothpick Man downs his drink.

TOOTHPICK MAN

You got more where that came from?

He puts his hand on her breast.

MAE/MOTHER

Of course.

She moves to get up, but he pulls her back down, kisses her mouth.

TOOTHPICK MAN

You taste good.

MAE/MOTHER

You've got good taste.

TOOTHPICK MAN

(in between kisses)

Now about that drink . . .

MAE/MOTHER

Coming right up. I'm well-stocked.

TOOTHPICK MAN

Well-stacked.

MAE/MOTHER

(laughs)

Mind yourself.

TOOTHPICK MAN

I don't mind myself at all. God, you're beautiful.

Mae/Mother's eyes fill with tears.

MAE/MOTHER

Why do I suddenly feel like lighting a candle?

TOOTHPICK MAN

(laughs)

You are. You're beautiful.

MAE/MOTHER

My daughter thinks I look like Mae West, except my hair's dark.

TOOTHPICK MAN

How does she know who Mae West is?

MAE/MOTHER

She's a weird kid.

TOOTHPICK MAN

When do I get to meet her?

MAE/MOTHER

You wanna meet my daughter?

TOOTHPICK MAN

Of course. Is she as beautiful as you?

MAE/MOTHER

(giggles)

You're a charmer. Actually, she looks more like her dad.

She's at the counter pouring, filling both glasses to the brim and spilling a little in the process.

TOOTHPICK MAN

How long were you married?

MAE/MOTHER

I wasn't. We weren't. We were planning to, once Velvet was born, but . . .

She takes a big drink.

TOOTHPICK MAN

But what?

MAE/MOTHER

He blew his brains out.

TOOTHPICK MAN

(softly)
Oh, babydoll . . .

MAE/MOTHER

Sorry. I didn't mean to tell you that. It's the gin.

Toothpick Man holds out his arms.

TOOTHPICK MAN

Come here.

MAE/MOTHER

I'm fine, really.

TOOTHPICK MAN

Baby, come here.

MAE/MOTHER

Do you want cheesecake?

INT. BRINKLEY'S HELL—MIRROR—
VELVET'S CHILDHOOD HOME—HALL STAIRS—CONTINUOUS

Velvet's eyes are dinner plates, her face bone-china-white.

VELVET

(frantic whisper)
Delilah, where are you? Delilah, come back! Delilah, cuddle me!

Tears fall from the plates, streak the china.

INT. BRINKLEY'S HELL—MIRROR—
VELVET'S CHILDHOOD HOME—BEDROOM—LATER

Velvet lies rigid and wide-awake in bed. Light from the hallway slices the dark through the slightly open door. Toothpick Man enters, letting in more light, and Velvet bolts upright and yanks her quilt around her, a threadbare armour. They stare at each other. Toothpick Man is naked.

TOOTHPICK MAN

Oh. I was looking for the bathroom. You must be the little lady of the house.

Velvet nods.

TOOTHPICK MAN

It's nice to meet you. You're pretty, just like your mom.

Long silence.

TOOTHPICK MAN

(looking around)

Nice room you got.

He notices the Dimetapp bottle sitting on the night table. He picks it up, and Velvet flattens herself against the wall.

TOOTHPICK MAN

You sick?

Velvet nods.

TOOTHPICK MAN

This stuff tastes good, doesn't it? I like the taste.

Long silence, while he stares at Velvet.

TOOTHPICK MAN

I'm gonna go find the bathroom now. You have sweet dreams, okay?

INT. VELVET'S HELL—MIRROR—BRINKLEY'S BEDROOM—NIGHT

Brinkley, in pinstriped pajamas and his peach angora sweater, paces the floor.

CLARA BOW

Hello, Brinkley. How's tricks?

He turns to Clara in the mirror.

CLARA BOW

Can't sleep neither? You can keep me company. My ma wore wooden clogs. Used ta stomp around all night.

BRINKLEY

My mother just moans all night.

CLARA BOW

Did she hold a knife to yer throat? My ma hates actresses, she thinks we're whores. She was just tryinta protect me. But I became the "It Girl" anyway, even though I'm kinda fat and I got red hair.

BRINKLEY

Red hair is the most beautiful. And you're not fat. You're perfect.

CLARA BOW

(teasing)

Ooh, so you're a cake-eater, are ya!

(pause, resigned)

Ah well, maybe Ma was right. We're all prostitutes anyway. Everybody's a whore to this life.

BRINKLEY

My mother never let me sleep. And now I'm awake forever. She always wanted to tell stories, or play dress-up, or go running outside in the middle of the night. I just want to sleep. My mother doesn't walk the floor anymore, she's too sick.

CLARA BOW

You're lyin'. Fess up.

BRINKLEY

What do you mean?

CLARA BOW

Yer mother ain't sick.

BRINKLEY

Yes she is. She moans all night long.

CLARA BOW

Liar! She don't moan all night, you do. You're keepin' yaself awake. She sleeps like a stone, drunk as the day is long.

BRINKLEY

You mean, she isn't really sick? She's not suffering?

CLARA BOW

How can she suffer when she's drunk? Lady *should* be sufferin', long and hard, if ya ask me. Wake up! Get a backbone! Solutions, Brinkley, solutions! Aren't men supposeta be good at fixin' things? Ha! That's a laugh!

(pause)

Listen kid, ya gotta help yaself.

BRINKLEY

Help myself? How?

CLARA BOW

Listen carefully.

BRINKLEY

What, Clara?

CLARA BOW

Nah, I'll tellya some other time. My mother entertained lotsa uncles.

BRINKLEY

Uncles?

CLARA BOW

Yeah, I got more uncles than any kid in the neighbourhood. She entertained, and I hid in the cupboard. 'S hardta breathe in there. Did you ever hide in a cupboard?

BRINKLEY

Yes.

CLARA BOW

When she was entertainin'?

BRINKLEY

No, when she was . . .

CLARA BOW

What?

BRINKLEY

Nothing. My mother loves me.

CLARA BOW

Whatever.

BRINKLEY

She does. I'm her special boy.

CLARA BOW

(chortles)

Yeah. You could call it that.

BRINKLEY

(screaming)

She does! She does! She does!

He collapses to the floor, tearing at his hair.

CLARA BOW

Brinkley! Brinkley! Brinkley!

He looks up at her, but remains on his knees, face full of tears.

CLARA BOW

What are ya gonna cry for, huh? That's *my* job.

BRINKLEY

(in a child's voice)

My mother loves me.

CLARA BOW

She loves ya too much. And not at all. My dad loves me too much. And I love him. But he goes away. He's too heavy for my little body. But he loves me.

BRINKLEY

(softly)

My mother is heavy too. She used to squish me and I couldn't breathe. It wasn't her fault, it's just that she drank a lot, because of my sister. She was always sad. And sometimes The Committee made her upset, when they weren't giving her good ideas for her paintings. The Committee kept changing the secret code, and she would get very frustrated and angry. I can understand why. But she is beautiful, like an angel. And sometimes she was fun, laughing. Sometimes she let me paint with her.

CLARA BOW

The fuckin' Committee's evil, that's what I think. Poisoned her mind. Just like Hollywood, if ya ask me. They treat me like garbage! I'm the goddamn "It Girl" and they treat me like trash!

(pause)

I wanna be an angel.

BRINKLEY

You *are* an angel.

CLARA BOW

Nobody helps me. I'm a great actress, but nobody helps me. They fish my storylines outta the wastepaper basket. And people say mean things about me. I'm a good girl, I am. No football teams, no football teams fer me. We was just friends. Fucking gossips. I'm one uh the boys, I am. My right's famous, back in Brooklyn.

BRINKLEY

I'll help you, Clara. My book is all for you. You're the best girl in the world.

CLARA BOW

I'm so lonely. All the time the flapper is laughin' and dancin', there's a feelin' of tragedy underneath.

BRINKLEY

(nodding)

I'm lonely too. I don't know how to talk to people. What to say. But I'd rather talk to you than anybody else in the whole world. I could dance with you, but I'm no good.

CLARA BOW

I was born durin' a heat wave. Brooklyn was fryin'. My ma hoped it'd kill us both, but we're not that lucky. She tried to kill ya, didn't she?

BRINKLEY

Who?

CLARA BOW

You know who.

Brinkley shakes his head, slow and glassy-eyed.

BRINKLEY

I have no idea what you are referring to.

CLARA BOW

Yer ma.

BRINKLEY

My mother is beautiful.

CLARA BOW

She triedta kill ya.

He shakes his head vigorously.

BRINKLEY

Never. Never. Never. Don't tell me that, Clara. Don't tell me that, Clara. Don't tell me that, Clara.

CLARA BOW

When you were a little kid.

Brinkley drops and curls into the fetal position, plugs his ears and screams.

CLARA BOW

Brinkley! Brinkley! Brinkley! Listenta me! Listenta me! Listenta me!

The screaming ceases, but the screamer remains curled like a snail shell on the floor.

CLARA BOW

Sit up. Look at me, little boy.

He remains on the floor.

CLARA BOW

Ya wanna see me cry?

Brinkley jumps to his feet.

BRINKLEY

(wipes his face)

Please don't cry, please don't cry!

CLARA BOW

Will ya stop screaming?

He nods.

CLARA BOW

How old were you?

Brinkley hangs his head, shakes it from side to side, covers his face.

CLARA BOW

Brinkley.

(gently)

Tell me. Tell me or I'll cry.

He drops his hands and looks at her. His whole body vibrates.

BRINKLEY

S-s-seven.

CLARA BOW

How?

BRINKLEY

She p-put-tt a-a p-pil-p-pilloww o-over m-my f-fa-ace.

CLARA BOW

Why did she stop?

BRINKLEY

B-be-cause sh-sh-e-e lo-loves m-mee.

CLARA BOW

I love you, Brinkley.

BRINKLEY

I-I lo-love y-you, C-Clara.

CLARA BOW

We're not gonna cry no more, you and me. I'm gonna help ya write yer book. We'll write a nice romance. You gonna dedicate it ta me?

BRINKLEY

(nodding)

I-It's all f-for y-you, C-Clara.

IO

My mirror—the movie oracle—had finished its show. (Can an oracle reveal the past, or only the future? In a place with no time, I guess the past and the future are one.) Brinkley's mother had once tried to kill him. And I was still trying to wrap my mind around the sight of a talking, living, breathing Clara Bow. I wondered again if his mother had been crazy before her daughter disappeared, or whether her insanity—and drinking habits—had been induced by trauma. I couldn't figure out whether being a veteran of the psych ward made me more of an authority on other people's craziness, or less. It takes one to know one, right?

I dropped to my knees and crawled to the wall, pressed my face against it, as though if I pressed hard enough I might pass through. If the mirror had let me into Brinkley's past, it had also let me into Brinkley's mind: I was in his bedroom with him, I saw what he saw. Clara spoke. So then she was real, if she was real to Brinkley. Since I saw what he saw, she was now real to me. (Wow, who'd have thought I'd get to see the "It Girl" of the '20s up close and personal? Davie would be going mental with jealousy if he knew—of course, he wouldn't be jealous of the fact that I'm stuck watching movies about a tragic germphobe, so I suppose I'm not really one up on him. Damn.) It'd always irked me how doctors outright dismissed the reality of people they couldn't see. What a limited and selfish perspective. Not to mention condescending. Reality is by its very nature subjective, to varying degrees. I think people like Brinkley and me simply have a more theatrical depth of field. A more kaleidoscopic viewfinder. And, unlike his mother, we never hurt anyone. But then again, I would tell myself all that stuff, my own personal highly abridged self-defence oration, privately titled "De Profundis of Craziness," but it never changed the fact that seeing things other people can't makes life very complicated. And lonely.

A cleaver of guilt hacked into my side, for having been so blunt about Brinkley's mother. But clearly she was abusive. Who tries to smother their kid with a pillow? And clearly he still loved her.

Pulling myself back to Homo erectus with the aid of the wall, I braved the mirror again. (Was this the modern incarnation of the Greek oracle? *Delphi: The Celluloid Version*. But if so, why wasn't it coughing up some prophecies? An oracle of the past is not all that helpful.) The atlas of bruises and scrapes on my body was gone. If anything, my skin appeared smoother, more even-toned, than I remembered. And it smelled of lavender. (Was I taking on the properties of the carpeting?) Running my hands over my arms and legs, I conducted an inspection, noted the near-absence of hair. The hairs that remained were soft, fine and blonde. Eyeball to armpit: same thing. I lifted up my dress—I was nine again. I still had hair on my head, although it was starting to thin and looked like I'd gone at it with a streaking kit—the mousy was spliced with shades of blonde. My eyebrows were fair, two slender brushstrokes, and my eyes still shone a clear gaze absent of impressions. It is a strange thing when you carry memory in your mind, and feel it in your bones, but you can't see it in your eyes.

Brinkley's letter in hand, I detoured to the bedroom door on my way to my writing desk and tried to open it. ('Twould be a terrible tragedy if I rotted in that room for Eternity, too distracted to notice that the door had become unlocked.) But alas, no such luck. I yanked until I was sure the knob was going to fly off, in fact was surprised that it didn't—everything in that place seemed to be Velvet-proofed—and then collapsed panting against smoothness.

At the desk I spread Brinkley's letter out in front of me, scrutinized the masculine blocky-ness of his handwriting. I liked the way he wrote my name. There was something bold and innocent about it, a certain possessive swagger coupled with self-conscious supplication. Seeing a man's handwriting was almost like seeing him naked. (Or maybe I'd just developed literary-themed perversions. The Shadowman had once told me that I was a naturally perverted person, but I don't really know what he was basing that on.) Brinkley entered the spotlight in my mind. I saw the half-smile, apologetic and wry, the generous nose and shy chin. I saw him with the green eyes I first knew, the ones that enclosed his life, not the alien blue. I heard his voice in my head as I read his letter.

Dear Velvet,

What can I write? (Besides some uncouth epistolary firebombs —FUCK YOU FUCK YOU FUCK YOU. I wore my mother's clothes because they made me feel close to the good parts of her. That's not sick. So there. All right. Now. Pause. Rewind. Dub over. Please forgive me. Please do not leave me.) I am the only one here to protect my mother. I was always the only one who could protect her, or try to. She does not love me anymore because . . . I cannot say. Perhaps she never did—there is certainly evidence to suggest that she loved my sister far more. But I don't like to dwell on that. I think she wanted me to become my sister, and I failed. I tried hard, though. It is impossible to live up to unreasonable expectations, but we do our best, correct? Your mirror will probably betray me, will probably let you see what a bad son I turned out to be, although I pray that it does not. If there is no God, does a prayer still make a sound? (I suppose that is a sad question. So why am I laughing so hard? I believe I may have what is known as a warped sense of humour. I also believe that this is something we share.)

I am truly, humbly sorry if my words caused you pain. Please do not leave me. Eternity is far too long to spend alone.

Perhaps you are correct, Velvet. Perhaps there is something liberating about craziness. Whatever craziness really is. However, my treasured relationship with Clara Bow certainly does not qualify me as crazy. I think it qualifies me as lucky. Not everyone has the pleasure of an intimate relationship with a movie star from the 1920s. Her visits with me were written into her contract. Perhaps other people might call me crazy, but they are merely limited in their perspective, so I do not take it personally.

Yes, my hair is turning colours. My eyebrows are so fair as to be almost invisible, and the hair on my head is a mixture of light and dark. Blond terror. Also, it is getting thinner. Here, as in life, the body betrays. But in reverse! Not only are my eyes and hair transforming, but my face seems younger, less definite. Lines disappearing. Perhaps that is part and parcel of the Hellish experience: you are returned to your original state, but forever kept from home—wherever that might be. But that would be assuming that infancy is our original state—a foolhardy thing to assume, no doubt.

Are you surprised that I wrote romance, not science fiction? (It is true; we may both be from Andromeda. Or who knows where. We are certainly not in a position to argue with any arcane possibilities.) You are surprised that I wrote romance at all, I know. As concerns science fiction, those books never sell without having a war or two, and I never liked weapons of any sort. My mother did. She liked violence. She was excited by it. Her paintings were always violent, with lots of red and black, lots of angry brushstrokes.

What happens to writing projects that are left unfinished? Do they die with you, or does someone else, in a sort of creative karmic passing of the torch, complete them? In ancient times, people believed words held magical power, that they were living beings, so it stands to reason that they would flap their wings and fly out in search of a mind to enshrine them. I hope whoever finishes my book takes good care of my characters.

I am not very adept at romance. But I always believed that if you watched enough movies, you would receive a celluloid approximation of life knowledge that could stand in for wisdom garnered firsthand. I have seen all the great romances. No leading lady has Clara Bow's fragile, urchin charm.

Yours very truly,

Brinkley

P.S. Yes, I am a Pisces.

P.P.S. Who do you like better: Gene Kelly or Fred Astaire?

Dear Brinkley,

I was about to write that you are overly sensitive, but instead I'll write what I really mean: you're a wimp. So Fuck You, too. (But keep the letters coming.) If you're going to announce to me that you had a thing for fine fabrics, and then I have to watch you in my mirror wearing those fine fabrics, I have a right to call it like I see it. So don't get your britches in a twist . . . or should I say panties? I'm not saying that your cross-dressing, wardrobe experimenting bothers me. *Au contraire*. But I'm not going to lie and tell you that wearing your mother's old clothes was a perfectly healthy thing to be doing. Besides, you already knew that you weren't embodying some aesthetic apex. So keep your cussing to yourself.

Frankly, you're a wimp about your mother, as well. (Good grief, I've seen this so many times before, though not to this severe a degree.) Your mother doesn't deserve your love or your protection. I know what she did to you when you were seven. You are safer here in Hell with me than you ever were with that woman. Maybe you're right—maybe she doesn't love you anymore. (Why wouldn't she? I can't believe you took care of her when she was sick!) So what?!!! Since I'm in the mood for blistering honesty, I may as well say: you're wise to assume she probably never did love you. You shouldn't love her, either. Who dresses their little boy up like a girl? How could she have expected you to fill your sister's sandals? Those weren't just impossible expectations, they were cruel. Oh, Brinkley. Why shoot your love at the wrong target, only to have it bounce back and hit you in the face?

I hadn't thought about whether someone back in life will finish my novella. Probably I should feel happy, thrilled and honoured that my creative intelligence might live on in the world, so of course I don't. I mean, I do want it to live on, but only with my name on the cover. The fact that I'm willing to express such selfish thoughts in Hell points to inherent stupidity in my personality. I've heard people say that suicide is a selfish act, but I think those people are short-sighted and judgmental. Anyway, I've been thinking, since I was bullied into killing myself by the Shadowman, wasn't my death actually a murder? Wouldn't God see that, if there is a God? Or will any attempt to evade responsibility be held against me? If there was a chance of getting out of here, I'm sure I've blown it. Pessimism is a nice cloak for other, greater personality flaws. It lets you pretend that you don't care to fix what's wrong. I'm so full of shit.

If I had lived, would I have finished my book? I ponder this over and over. Of course, the list of eternal ponderings grows ever longer: would I have married, would I have gotten up the nerve to go skinny-dipping despite gravity's hostile takeover, would I have visited Paris and retraced Audrey Hepburn and Cary Grant's footsteps? I'm guessing the answer is no to the first question, and maybe to the other two. Would the Shadowman have one day left me alone for good? Would I have missed the sick bastard if he had? We're attached to the familiar, even if we don't like it. And he was nice to me sometimes. I appreciated his fashion sense. The thing about the Shadowman is, he's kind of a genius in his own right. He gave me lots of creative ideas of all sorts. An unfinished book is an open wound. This room is full of festers. Can a genius know they are a genius, or does such self-knowledge disqualify them? I wonder if I could've been a genius. Schopenhauer said that women are incapable of genius. Of course, he was an idiot—the easy, flippant, dismissive, and necessary response. But his assertion bothered me, kept me awake, pestered me while I served curries. He said that women may be talented, but genius will always elude them because they are distracted by biological creativity. The truth is that women have access to more forms of genius than men, and so men are desperate to discount us and stake their claim. That doesn't answer the question of whether I could've been a genius, though in all likelihood the answer is no.

I would write my book here, if I had enough paper. But given the choice between writing my book and writing to you, I choose you. Funny, on so many nights I sat at my desk, stumped and wordless, plotless, trimming split ends with nail scissors and imagining what the book's cover would look like, wondering how many people would buy it. Now that I'm here, words hitch themselves together to form sentences in my mind and I long to finish it, even though no other soul will ever know what it says.

Sincerely, Velvet

P.S. I used to think that nothing compared to Gene Kelly in *Singin' in the Rain*. But then he severely traumatized me. Or the Shadowman did, wearing a Gene Kelly disguise. So maybe I'm more of an Astaire girl, after all.

Dear Velvet,

I have been trying to think of a more creative way to express my anger, since I already used "Fuck You" more than once, and it is such an overused expression. But the word "Fuck" combined with the word "You" expresses my sentiments so perfectly. Perhaps I am a wimp. So? You are hardly in a position to criticize. I love my mother and I love Clara Bow, and I want them to love me too. (I am sure Clara wonders where I have gone. This thought haunts me.) You will never understand. Yes, my mother did a bad thing to me when I was seven, but she stopped. She did not know what she was doing. And I believe it's possible to save someone by killing them.

Killing can be an act of kindness. So perhaps in her heart, when she put the pillow over my face, she was being kind. And I'll tell you a secret: sometimes, I wished that she had gone through with it. Only during the times when Clara Bow was not around, and I had no one else. A lonely path is a tiring path. I think my mother was lonely, with only bad memories for company. I had a duty to her: duty is the practical execution of love. Clara had a particular idea of what that duty entailed, but I do not believe now that she was correct. Given my circumstances, I know that she was not.

I think it is fair to wonder whether you were indeed murdered by the Shadowman. He compelled you, after all, so would he not be convicted in court, at least as an accessory? Not that I can lay claim to extensive knowledge of legalities, but in your case there were most definitely mitigating circumstances.

Whether I am a wimp or not is immaterial: do not ever criticize my love for anyone. Your Eternity in that bedroom will be lonely without my letters.

Since you like "blistering" honesty: I know what really happened to your dad. I am sorry, Velvet. Do you think some legacies are inescapable? Perhaps the Shadowman stalked your father, also. What a murderous demon.

Your novella will see the light, if it is meant to. Though I always thought these things would cease to be of any concern after one had died. The Divine Dissatisfaction of the artist keeps us marching forward, even if we cannot march far. My mother's painting life was constantly consumed by frustration. Dissatisfaction was certainly her lot. I saw her destroy many of her paintings with an X-acto knife. And other things too, like wallpaper. She liked to destroy as much as she liked to create. Perhaps destruction and creativity felt the same to her. You are correct, she should not have dressed me up like a girl, and I never much cared for it when she did. Grief is a poison. It was not until I was older that I came to enjoy women's clothing. The softness of it, like a security blanket.

I remember standing on my bed in the middle of the night when I was a kid, looking out the window at the street below and the stars above. Already I loved Clara Bow (through her movies, only—she did not come to visit me until I was older), already I loved Marlowe and would recite his lines to myself whenever I was alone. On those nights, looking out at the world from my bedroom, I felt myself expand, so full of possibility. How quickly the world absorbs us, and we forget where we are going. Or perhaps we never really knew.

Yours very truly,

Brinkley

P.S. Astaire and Ginger, those were the days. I do not blame you for swearing off Gene Kelly after the Shadowman appropriated his raincoat.

Dear Brinkley,

All right. Fine. Truce. (For the record, I don't think I have to worry about you stopping your letters. An empty threat. You would be just as lonely as me. No one else is accepting your mail.) We don't seem to have an endless supply of paper, and there's no sense in using it up fighting about things that are irrelevant now.

My mother always insisted that my father had been hit by a car. (An existential car, perhaps? A meaningless Mustang with no muffler? And if she was going to lie to me, why didn't she think up a better lie than that?) So if the topic ever came up, I always insisted the same. But I know what really happened. Clearly, some legacies are inescapable. And you're right, the Shadowman may have targeted my dad first, and after doing away with him, eventually fixated on me.

I never was an optimist; that much is obvious. But you have given me hope. Because even though you're a wimp, you're a good wimp. Someone as good as you could never be left here for Eternity. Even if I deserve this fate, I refuse to believe that you do.

I thought I was going to Heaven, thought I would meet my dad. (Maybe he's locked in the room next door. Does irony exist in Hell?) But given the circumstances, the pain I have caused those I love, I see now that I was far too generous with myself in expecting that there would be any measure of mercy for me. I could've tried harder to resist the Shadowman's threats. Your case is entirely different, though. If this is Hell, then Heaven must exist and there must be a place in it for you. I am terrified that you will leave me. Terrified, and yet I hope, for your sake, that I'm right.

Memories are the living monsters of this place. Everything in this room reminds me of what used to be, and everything in my mind is scourging me from the inside out. I remember staying with my mother and her then-boyfriend in a cabin by the sea. From the beach I would gather buckets of shells and then sit on the deck in the hot afternoons to lay them out in patterns. I remember the smell of sun on the wood cabin mixed with the salt from the sea, a heavy, warm, sad smell, the scent of tears. The shells, mostly broken, joined to form jagged hearts. Sometimes a small star. An unoriginal artist, I was. My mother and her boyfriend mostly stayed out of the heat, sitting inside in front of a fan, drinking beer and eating salted peanuts. I used to have dreams about Mr. Peanut dancing with me like Gene Kelly, and I often made my own monocle by biting the centre out of a cucumber slice. One evening my mother had too much to drink and went swimming, and nearly drowned. Her boyfriend had to rescue her. I sat on the deck watching them lying on the sand, her gasping and choking. Funny, I didn't run down to the beach. I remember feeling like there was concrete in my shoes and in my hands. All I kept thinking was: I wish Delilah was here, I wish she had come with us. (She'd moved away, and we lost touch.)

Do we really love the people we think we love?

Sincerely, Velvet

P.S. I caught myself humming "As Time Goes By." Irony reaches new heights.

Dear Velvet,

My mother has her reasons, I am sure, for being satisfied with my current predicament. But I am confused as to why the Powers That Be have not recognized my noble intentions, have not recognized that I took care of her much more than she ever took care of me. She was a beautiful woman, so beautiful that even I, the one who saw her every day, could look at her and miss a breath. Well, I do not have to tell you, you have seen her. Perhaps every man's mother assumes mythological proportions that refuse to be diminished. Beautiful people can be deadly. I think she often wondered how it was that she produced such a physically inferior child, and I always wondered why it was that God failed to outfit her with the biological blinders that so many parents wear, the ones that cause them to regard an average-looking child as beautiful, and to see the promise of genius in the child's ability to stack blocks. She used to speak often of how beautiful my sister was, but she didn't keep any photographs of her around.

I was hit by a car and then I arrived here, without fanfare. I have said all that I can say about my mother and her feelings about me. If your mirror chooses to reveal anything else—it is out of my hands. Of course I was a sinner, but I tried hard, cobbled together an effort toward goodness, believing all the while that God was not as picky as God is at present demonstrating Itself to be. But maybe the concept of "trying" is really what is most hateful to the Higher-Up, such a pathetically human sweat- and tear-covered automatically self-excusing notion. If mercy were mine to give, I would lay it at your feet.

Memory is a ghoulish machine and the cog of memory is regret. I will not be missed by many on Earth and this realization is scorching. But I think Clara misses me. I need to believe that. So I mattered to one person. Perhaps that is all we need. I think I matter to you, now. Clara was hard on me and perhaps a wee bit misguided in some of her advice, but I could depend on her to appear with some regularity. Dependability is a great quality in a friend. She was always there for me, and I could tell her all my troubles. We would talk about cinema and the difficulties inherent in transitioning from silents to talkies. When I was with Clara, I never felt lonely.

Yours very truly,

Brinkley

P.S. Which Fred Astaire bit is your favourite?

INT. BRINKLEY'S HELL—MIRROR—
VELVET'S CHILDHOOD HOME—KITCHEN—MORNING

Velvet sits at the kitchen table. Mae/Mother dances at the stove, sprinkling dill onto an omelette. She belts out "Fly Me to the Moon."

Velvet watches her, stone-faced. She gets up and goes to a cupboard, retrieves dishes and cutlery and sets the table for three.

MAE/MOTHER

Oh Vee, he's a dream! A dream! What do you think? Should I really go blonde?

She carries the frying pan to the table and places an omelette on Velvet's plate.

MAE/MOTHER

Why did you set the table for three? He had to leave early this morning.

(giggles)

But he'll be back!

VELVET

I set a place for Delilah, in case she comes back.

MAE/MOTHER

Huh? Oh, didn't know she was missing.

VELVET

She went missing yesterday.

MAE/MOTHER

Jesus, Velvet, you're carrying this imaginary friend thing a bit far. Get some real friends.

Velvet starts screaming.

MAE/MOTHER

Velvet! Velvet!

VELVET

(screaming)

I want Delilah! I want Delilah! I want Delilah!

Mae/Mother slaps her. Silence, like a box, shuts Velvet in. Then come the tears.

MAE/MOTHER

Oh honey, I'm sorry, I'm sorry, Mommy's sorry, you were hysterical, you have to slap hysterical people, I saw it in a movie! Oh, don't cry, don't cry, no reason to cry!

Mae/Mother rocks her back and forth.

MAE/MOTHER

Eat your omelette, baby. I put dill in it, just the way you like. How 'bout some cookies, too? I bought the ones with Smarties in them.

She runs to a cookie jar on the counter and brings it to the table.

MAE/MOTHER

Does Delilah want a cookie?

VELVET

Delilah's not here. She moved away. I don't know where. And she hates Smarties.

MAE/MOTHER

Oh. Well, more for us then, right? Eat your omelette, Vee. No more screaming. It's a beautiful, beautiful, glorious, fabulous, wonderful day!

(giggles to herself)

He'll be back, oh yes, he'll be back . . .

VELVET

What happened to my dad?

Mae/Mother is still. A moment passes.

MAE/MOTHER

(slowly)

I told you what happened. There was an accident.

VELVET

You said something else. I heard you say something else.

MAE/MOTHER

No, Velvet. You must've been dreaming.

VELVET

I heard what you said. I heard you.

MAE/MOTHER

There was an accident. He was hit by a car. You know this. I've told you. He loved you, Vee. Pinky swear.

Velvet is silent. She stares at her lap.

MAE/MOTHER

Honey . . .

VELVET

(looks up suddenly)

I don't like your date.

MAE/MOTHER

(sharply)

What? You haven't even met him.

Velvet shrugs.

MAE/MOTHER

Eat your omelette.

VELVET

I don't want my omelette.

MAE/MOTHER

Then starve.

Silence.

VELVET

I'll have a cookie.

MAE/MOTHER

Fine then. Have a cookie.

**INT. BRINKLEY'S HELL—MIRROR—
VELVET'S CHILDHOOD HOME—BEDROOM—NIGHT**

Velvet lies in bed, staring at the ceiling. Her bedroom door opens. She sits up.

VELVET

Delilah?

The Toothpick Man enters.

TOOTHPICK MAN

Hi there, little lady. Thought I'd stop by and say hello. I was just on my way to the bathroom.

**INT. BRINKLEY'S HELL—MIRROR—
VELVET'S CHILDHOOD HOME—BEDROOM—LATER**

Velvet is sitting up in bed writing Roman numerals in a notebook by the light of her bedside lamp. She tears the page from her notebook and fashions it into a paper airplane, then gets out of bed and drags a chair to the window. Once balanced on the chair, she opens the window and stares at the moon, a lidless, sightless eye. She aims her paper plane toward it, and sends it on its red-eye flight.

VELVET

(softly)

Delilah. Come back.

INT. VELVET'S HELL—MIRROR—BRINKLEY'S BEDROOM—NIGHT

Clara sways, grace emanating like candle flame.

CLARA BOW

(sings)

"Sleep my love and peace attend thee

All through the night . . .
Guardian angels God will lend thee
All through the night . . .
Soft the drowsy hours are creeping
Hill and dale in slumber steeping
Love alone his watch is keeping
All through the night . . ."

Brinkley dances, a slow shuffle.

CLARA BOW

That's a corking good song. I'm so glad ya taught it ta me. Doesn't put me ta sleep, but still a nice song.

BRINKLEY

When you sing, my mind is clear. I have no memories.

CLARA BOW

That's like when I act. No memories. I don't believe in the past or the future, I only believe in right now.

BRINKLEY

I like that philosophy. You are a wise woman.

CLARA BOW

Ya needta distract yaself. A good death scene is the best distraction.

BRINKLEY

You were the best die-er ever. Your final scene in *Children of Divorce* should be canonized.

CLARA BOW

No pope's gonna canonize a movie, 'specially not one called *Children of Divorce*.

BRINKLEY

My mother was crying again this morning.

CLARA BOW

So how ya gonna help yaself? Ya wanna listenta her whinin' the rest uh yer life?

BRINKLEY

I don't know how to help myself! My nervous pills aren't working! I hate the racket she makes! What should I do? Tell me!

CLARA BOW

I can't tell ya, baby. Ya gotta figure it out on yer own. The answer's right in front uh you. Simple as can be. You'll figure it out. Trust me, baby. Take it from me, the best die-er in the business.

BRINKLEY

I tried playing *Gilda* for her. That's her favourite movie. But she threw her glass at the television. My heart hurts, Clara. And my head.

CLARA BOW

(shrugs)

That's what a heart does. Damn thing won't stop. World could blow up and there'd be a buncha hearts left ovah, still tickin', feelin' the pain.

BRINKLEY

May I kiss you?

CLARA BOW

Fer you, I got plenty uh kisses.

Brinkley approaches her cautiously, then stops short.

CLARA BOW

You're a shy one, aren't ya? I love that. Just like a little boy I loved.

BRINKLEY

A little boy?

CLARA BOW

My little friend who lived downstairs. He burned to death, right in front uh me. His mother screamin' like a crazy person, not doin' nothin' 'bout it. I triedta put 'im out but . . .

(starts to cry)

Kiss me quick, Brinkley, kiss me quick!

He kisses her, tentative and tender.

CLARA BOW

Ya look just like 'im.

(starting to fall apart)

I loved him, I loved him, I loved him, I loved him!

BRINKLEY

Don't cry, don't cry! I love you, I love you, I love you!

CLARA BOW

I love ya too, kid. But ya gotta stop bein' such a wimp. Yer ma deserves 'er sufferin', that's what I say. Lady's a fuckin' bitch. But you, you shouldn't hafta suffer. You're an angel.

BRINKLEY

Do you really think so? I would not let anyone else say that about her, but you're special. I know you think she's crazy. I have tried to be a good son. One time she burned me with a cigarette, when she'd had too much to drink. But I believe it was an accident. She could be so kind when she was happy, so creative. We built lots of forts together. And watched movies. We watched *Gilda* every Sunday, like a religion.

CLARA BOW

Yer ma's definitely crazy, hate ta break it to ya. But you got yer head on straight. Ya done right by 'er, no question. Took care uh her like nobody else woulda.

```
It's time fer you ta be free. So if ya don't want
the bitch around anymore, then put on yer thinkin'
cap, kid.
```

Dear Brinkley,

You're right: Clara Bow is the most beautiful movie star in the world. But somehow the most frightening. Seeing you together in the mirror terrifies me. Maybe we shouldn't talk about the movie memories anymore. I don't know what you're seeing on your mirror/movie screen, but probably I don't want to be reminded. Then again, what else do we have to talk about, other than the fact that we're looking more freakish by the minute, or I am, anyway. Clara is a tough cookie. I admire that about her. Wish I'd been tougher. Tough enough to kick the Shadowman in the balls. I used to let Davie walk all over me, too. But I admired his bravado, wanted some of it to rub off on me. And he was loyal, I'll give him that. He wasn't afraid of me.

I have to say that I agree with Clara Bow's assessment of your mother, although I know you're willing to take it from her and not from me. So I'm not trying to start an argument. I just understand why you love Clara so much, because it's like she gets to say all the things you can't. Sort of like me and the Shadowman, only I hate him and he terrifies me, a lot of the time. But he does say lots of things that other people maybe wouldn't, gets to wear lots of costumes that other people don't. Maybe I'm jealous of him, because he is free to be as mean as he wants—he always gets away with it.

The Shadowman hasn't shown up here lately, which is weird considering I'm in Hell. Since he often made my life on Earth rather hellish, I'd expect him to be camping out in this room fulltime. I should shut my mouth, 'cause next thing you know he'll make an entrance and I'll have deviled egg on my face—ha ha, bad pun, sincere apologies. I've learned that the other shoe is always about to drop.

Here's the last thing I'll say (for a while, anyhow) about your colourful painter of a mother: If she did indeed burn you with one of her ever-present cigarettes, I doubt very much that it was an accident and therefore when the time was right, you should have snuck up on her and put a pillow over her face once and for all. That's just my opinion and I'm not saying it to upset you, I'm saying it because I like you a lot.

I used to have recurring dreams that I was a Victorian-era scribe ravaged by TB. Oh, why couldn't I have been born way earlier and died of consumption instead?!! Maybe I shouldn't have read so much poetry. I think it should come with a Surgeon General's Warning. Not that there is a direct, provable link between poetry and suicide, but you do have to travel the depths to come up with some decent lines, and not everyone who goes down comes up. Obviously, the same is true of prose as well, as evidenced by me. But it really wasn't writing that killed me, it was the Shadowman. The thing is, he's so creative that I probably got all my best inspirations—and therefore a measure of happiness—from him.

I've taken another "escape hatch inventory" of my room. This place makes Fort Knox look like Legoland.

I also, in a fit of despair, plucked all the eyes out of the stuffed animals that are sitting on the bed, staring (formerly staring) at me dumbly. Now I'm wracked with remorse. The eyes are the window to the soul, and I just broke all the windows. Not that stuffed animals have souls, but they have pretend-souls and that's better than nothing. And let's face it, maybe I don't have a soul, either. If I do, it's probably like my brain: a doily. In other words, a lot of holes in it and not very useful.

Sincerely, Velvet

P.S. Even though it's not a fancy dance sequence, the Fred Astaire bit I loved best was in *Funny Face*, the part when he sings "'S Wonderful" with Audrey Hepburn.

Dear Velvet,

Do you have any psychic ability? If you do, I hope that you will keep on liking me. If you do not, then I suppose the mirror will eventually convict me anyway. The beautiful, as I stated, can be dangerous. I followed Clara's advice and chose not to be a wimp. Justice is noble. You are right, Velvet: perhaps we should not discuss what we see in the mirror. Bad things happen, and when the movie is over sometimes it is best to forget. On second thought, I second your second thought: avoidance seems silly. What we witness in the mirror must form the crux of our correspondence. When one is in Hell, what is the point of avoiding bad things? Badness is the inevitability of our circumstance.

I have a terrible feeling that the Final Judgment is yet to come. I keep searching about for signs of heat.

I am happy that you admire Clara's toughness, as I do. She really keeps me in line. I always kept my relationship with her private, as I did not want the interference of outsiders. Also because Clara is famous, and she asked for my discretion. We both are attracted to gutsy people, perhaps finding courage lacking in ourselves. There is something thrilling about people who are willing to speak their mind, to grab hold of their meanness with both hands. Something brave about ugliness.

If you live in a black-and-white film world, what can be done? Nothing. I always knew that there were only two things in life that brought me happiness: classic cinema and Clara Bow. So I played my scenes with her and kept moving. Now that we have heard "Cut" and found a thespian's retirement lacking, we are forced to enter into endless and despairing debates about souls. We have souls, Velvet. No use though, no use. I never liked horror films.

Yours very truly,

Brinkley

P.S. Since you were not a silent film buff I cannot ask you questions about those, so tell me this: which is the best movie song, "As Time Goes By" or "Moon River"?

INT. BRINKLEY'S HELL—MIRROR—
VELVET'S CHILDHOOD HOME—BACKYARD—NIGHT

Velvet and Mae/Mother sit on a blanket on the grass, staring at the winking beyonds. A small table nearby is covered with candles; they heft their shivering petals of flame to the sky. Mae/Mother's hair is platinum blonde.

MAE/MOTHER

Big Dipper, Little Dipper. Where's Cassiopeia's Chair? Oh, that's what I want when I die, my own chair made of stars. Wouldn't that be divine, Vee?

(silence)
Vee?

VELVET
I'm connecting the stars, making Roman numerals. I'm up to eleven.

MAE/MOTHER
Well, maybe one of your Roman numerals has a special star in it, a star just for you.

She looks at Velvet, her face starlit with eagerness, a child with a cupcake and a secret.

VELVET
What are you talking about?

MAE/MOTHER
I bought you a star for your birthday!

VELVET
What?

MAE/MOTHER
(points)
That one. I'm pretty sure it's that one.

VELVET
You can't buy a star. Heaven is free.

MAE/MOTHER
Yes you can! Isn't it the greatest birthday present ever?

VELVET
You're joking.

MAE/MOTHER
I never joke about astronomy.

VELVET

You really bought me a star?

MAE/MOTHER

Cross my heart and kiss my kneecap.

VELVET

Show me again.

MAE/MOTHER

I think it's that bright one, above the Big Dipper.

VELVET

It's part of my number nine!

MAE/MOTHER

See! It's meant to be yours!

VELVET

Cross your heart and kiss your kneecap.

Mae/Mother does. Velvet looks up in wonderment.

VELVET

That's really my star. It's so beautiful.

MAE/MOTHER

Velvet is the perfect name for a star. Much better than the Big Dipper. Well, I guess that's a bunch of stars, but still.

VELVET

None of the other kids at school have their own star.

MAE/MOTHER

Of course not. Only very special birthday girls get a piece of Heaven. Are you gonna show it to your friend?

VELVET

What friend?

MAE/MOTHER

You know, what's her face . . .

VELVET

Delilah?

MAE/MOTHER

Yeah, her.

VELVET

Remember, she's gone.

MAE/MOTHER

Gone where?

VELVET

I don't know. She moved. She didn't leave a forwarding address.

MAE/MOTHER

Oh.

Velvet starts to cry. Her face is tilted up, toward her star.

MAE/MOTHER

Baby.

VELVET

I miss her. I want her to come back.

MAE/MOTHER

Oh dollface, no birthday tears. I'm sure she'll come back. Then again, maybe it's a sign that you're too old for pretend-friends. Maybe she went to find somebody younger.

Velvet cries harder.

MAE/MOTHER

(throwing her arms around Velvet)

Babydoll, my sweet as sugar, don't cry, don't cry, I bought you a star, nobody with their own star can be sad, it's against the rules, the Milky Way rules. Ssshhh . . . I love you, love you, love you, my precious—Oh my God! Doorbell, I heard a doorbell! He's here! How do I look? Okay? Wipe your face!

She goes flying into the house. Velvet stares at the sky.

INT. BRINKLEY'S HELL—MIRROR—
VELVET'S CHILDHOOD HOME—FRONT HALL—CONTINUOUS

Mae/Mother rips open the front door and leaps into the arms of Toothpick Man, wrapping her legs around him with cobra force. He staggers under her weight. She devours his mouth, a ravenous carnivore.

TOOTHPICK MAN
(trying to wrench free)
Easy, darlin', easy. Someone missed me.

He drops the stuffed animal he was carrying. Mae/Mother dives for it, squealing like a child at a petting zoo.

MAE/MOTHER
Ooh, for me! So cute! What a sweetie!

She moves to fling herself at Toothpick Man once again.

TOOTHPICK MAN
Whoa, easy honey, it's not for you, it's for the birthday girl.

MAE/MOTHER
(pouting)
Oh. Fine then.

She drops the animal.

MAE/MOTHER

Nothing for me?

TOOTHPICK MAN

Well.

(winks at her)

Maybe something for you. I'll show you later.

He grabs her ass and she squeals. Her squeal becomes a giggle, which descends into a rough contralto come-hither rumble. She puts his fingers in her mouth and sucks, her wet gaze unflickering.

TOOTHPICK MAN

(touching her platinum hair)

You really do look exactly like Mae West.

She moves his hand out of her mouth and onto her breast.

TOOTHPICK MAN

Later, baby. After cake.

INT. BRINKLEY'S HELL—MIRROR—VELVET'S CHILDHOOD HOME—KITCHEN DOORWAY TO BACKYARD—CONTINUOUS

Toothpick Man stands in the doorway to the backyard and calls to Velvet, who still sits on the grass.

TOOTHPICK MAN

Happy Birthday, little lady! Brought a present for you! Come and get it!

Velvet stands and walks slowly toward him. As she passes, the candle flames flick like tongues.

TOOTHPICK MAN

Happy Birthday, sweetheart!

He scoops her up. Velvet is rigid, her face the inscrutable

mask of a wooden doll. Toothpick Man kisses her cheek, sets her down and hands her the stuffed animal.

TOOTHPICK MAN

(calling into the kitchen)

Your daughter gets prettier every time I see her.

(touches her face)

Don't you, little lady? Let's have some cake.

INT. BRINKLEY'S HELL—MIRROR—
VELVET'S CHILDHOOD HOME—KITCHEN—CONTINUOUS

Velvet and Toothpick Man sit at the table while Mae/ Mother swoops in carrying a chocolate cake and singing at eardrum-rattling volume.

MAE/MOTHER

Happy Birthday to you,
You live in a zoo!
Happy Birthday, dear Vee Vee,
Happy Birthday to you!

She sets it down with a twirl and a curtsy.

MAE/MOTHER

Blow, blow, blow!

TOOTHPICK MAN

Steady as she blows!

The two adults look at each other and dissolve into hysterical laughter. Velvet stares at her candles.

MAE/MOTHER

Make a wish, a juicy wish!

Velvet blows out the flames. Mae/Mother claps wildly and jumps up and down, her vampish figure brimming with bounce and shake. Toothpick Man hoists a drink.

TOOTHPICK MAN

To the prettiest birthday girl in the world!

Mae/Mother stops jumping, and her wobbly flesh comes to an abrupt halt. Her smile is gone. She snatches her drink from the table and downs it.

MAE/MOTHER

(loudly)

Aren't these flowers gorgeous?

(indicating irises on the table)

I was in a Van Gogh mood.

TOOTHPICK MAN

Hope you wished for something really good, Velvet.

MAE/MOTHER

Yeah, hope you didn't waste it on world peace.

TOOTHPICK MAN

So what did you get for your birthday?

VELVET

A star.

TOOTHPICK MAN

A star?

He looks to Mae/Mother. She shrugs.

MAE/MOTHER

(airily)

I bought her a star. Show 'im, Vee.

Velvet gets up and goes into the backyard. Toothpick Man follows her.

VELVET

(points)

I think it's that one.

TOOTHPICK MAN

Prettiest star for the prettiest girl. You get anything else for your birthday?

VELVET

Press-on nails.

Mae/Mother stands in the doorway, illuminated by the light from the kitchen like some burlesque avenging angel. Her hair looks white.

MAE/MOTHER

Can't get through life without press-on nails.

(drinks)

Can you, Vee Vee?

INT. BRINKLEY'S HELL—MIRROR—
VELVET'S CHILDHOOD HOME—BEDROOM—LATER

The lamp on the night table warms the room. Velvet stands on a chair and blows on her window, writes Roman numerals in the steam. Carnal shrieking reverberates: the sounds of mortal combat. Both fighters are conquered: a final gasp, silence. Velvet's finger squeaks as she writes. Beneath her row of numbers, she traces the name "Delilah."

INT. BRINKLEY'S HELL—MIRROR—
VELVET'S CHILDHOOD HOME—BEDROOM—LATER

Velvet is asleep. As though yanked from a dream by her ponytail she sits up, turns on the lamp. Toothpick Man is in the doorway, clad only in his underwear. He teeters slightly, as though standing on a balance beam for the first time.

TOOTHPICK MAN

Hi there, little l-lady. I was just on my way to the bathroom and I wanted to say . . . Happy Birthday.

He staggers into the room, closing the door behind him. His shadow is huge on the wall. Velvet is motionless in bed, her eyes fixed orbs.

TOOTHPICK MAN

You're the prettiest little girl in the world. Do you know that? I think you do. I think you know that. Don't you? Don't you?

Velvet shakes her head. His shadow is huge on the wall. He moves to the bed.

TOOTHPICK MAN

Say it. Say "I am the prettiest little girl in the world." Say it.

Velvet stares at the window, at her Roman numerals and the name "Delilah."

VELVET

(whispers)

Delilah, Delilah, Delilah, Delilah, Delilah, Delilah.

His shadow is huge on the wall.

INT. VELVET'S HELL—MIRROR—
BRINKLEY'S BEDROOM—NIGHT

Brinkley stands before his mirror dressed in women's clothing and shuffling recipe cards. He is anxious, consumed by his thoughts. Clara Bow appears in the mirror, steps out of it.

CLARA BOW

Brinkley!

He jerks into cognizance.

BRINKLEY

What, what, what is it? Oh, Clara! Thank God you're here. I'm nervous. Scared, I'm scared.

CLARA BOW

Whatcha gotta be scared of, huh? We been ovah everythin' awready.

BRINKLEY

I forget.

CLARA BOW

Whaddya mean ya forget? Ya got amnesia or somethin'?

BRINKLEY

No. I have recipe cards.

CLARA BOW

And why do you got recipe cards?

BRINKLEY

So I won't forget.

CLARA BOW

Well they sure as hell aren't fer writin' recipes on! I can't cook nothin', 'cept stewed prunes. I can stew a prune like nobody's business. So hurry up, get a pen!

Brinkley rushes to his desk. He plucks a Kleenex from his Cotswold cottage Kleenex dispenser and blows his nose. Then he takes a pen from a brass penholder and returns to the mirror. He shuffles his recipe cards, drops half.

CLARA BOW

Are we gonna be here all night? I could make a movie in less time. Come to think of it, I *did* make a movie in less time.

BRINKLEY

P-please, Clara. I-I'm nervous.

CLARA BOW

Nothin' ta be nervous about. You're doin' right, sweetheart. You get to be there. You get to be there when she goes. When all her pain goes. And yers. 'Course, ya know what I think uh her. Yer doin' both uh you a favour. Just be happy ya get to see 'er off. I never got ta do that. I was dancin' on a table when my ma went. I think I killed her.

BRINKLEY

You didn't kill her!

CLARA BOW

Yes I did. She disapproved of me. Thought I was a whore. An actress whore. And there I was, dancin' on a table.

BRINKLEY

Clara?

CLARA BOW

Yeah?

BRINKLEY

Am I a killer?

CLARA BOW

No, Brinkley. Yer a man with recipe cards. And yer gonna set her free.

BRINKLEY

Free.

CLARA BOW

Free. Besides, remember what happened with the cigarette? Remember when she dressed you up like a girl? Now ya like dressin' like a girl sometimes, but ya didn't when she was pickin' the clothes. And remember when she was drunk and crazy? Remember how heavy she was? Ya couldn't breathe! Now pick up yer cards.

Brinkley bends to gather the spilt cards and, in doing so, drops all of them. His hands are shaky, and he dabs with the cuffs of his fluffy sweater at the sweat dewing his hairline. It takes him quite some time to organize himself.

CLARA BOW

Ya ready?

He stands, neatening the edges of his stack of cards, and poises his pen.

BRINKLEY

Yes.

CLARA BOW

Find a blue pillow.

He writes, "Step #1: Find a blue pillow" on the top recipe card.

BRINKLEY

What is Step #2?

Clara is suddenly agitated and distracted, paces the floor.

CLARA BOW

I shoulda found a blue pillow, stuck it ovah my father's face. Instead I brought him to set with me, treated him like a goddamn king. I must be stupid!

(increasingly upset)

I must be as crazy as he was! Nobody loves me, nobody loves me, nobody loves me, nobody loves me, nobody loves me!

BRINKLEY

I love you, Clara! Please don't forget about me!

CLARA BOW

(ranting)

Everythin' hurts and I can't sleep and the pills don't

work and the doctors say I'm a hypochondriac but I'm not! Nobody believes me, nobody listens tuh me!

BRINKLEY

I listen! I listen to everything you say. I hurt too. But my mother hurts more. She hurts so much. Which makes me feel happy. But that's our secret, right? I play *Gilda* for her every day but she just cries and talks to herself. It's hard to sleep with all the noise she makes. But I don't really sleep anyway.

Clara is calm. She sports a steely look.

CLARA BOW

Make a triple scotch.

BRINKLEY

What?

CLARA BOW

Step #2: Make a triple scotch.

BRINKLEY

I don't drink.

CLARA BOW

Not fer you, stupid. For her.

BRINKLEY

Oh, yes of course, she likes scotch very much. Very much indeed.

(as he writes)

"Make a triple scotch." Then what?

CLARA BOW

Get a small bowl of salt.

BRINKLEY

A bowl of salt? What for?

CLARA BOW

Do ya want me tuh tell ya what to do or not?

BRINKLEY

I'm sorry, Clara, so sorry. Please go ahead.

CLARA BOW

All right, then. Get a wet cloth, some Aspirin and a jar of dill pickles.

He scribbles notes on his recipe cards.

CLARA BOW

When in a pickle, eat a pickle! That's good advice. My favourite food is Chinese, though. That's the next step. Order Chinese food.

BRINKLEY

What should I order?

CLARA BOW

Chop suey, chow mein, egg rolls and wonton soup. Oh, and make sure they give ya extra fortune cookies. We gotta read our fortunes. But I think I awready know what happens tuh me.

BRINKLEY

You stay beautiful forever. And we live happily ever after.

CLARA BOW

(exploding)

Nobody lives happily ever after! That's bullshit! Bullshit! Bullshit! Bullshit! Bullshit!

(cries)

Oh, I can't take care uh my boys, I love my boys, I love 'em, love 'em, I love 'em! I need ta be alone. I'm so scared all the time. So scared. So scared.

Brinkley reaches out and takes her hand.

BRINKLEY

Just stay with me. We can take care of each other.

CLARA BOW

(nodding, calming down)

Okay. I'll stay with you. I'll stay with you. I'll stay with you. I gotta pull myself togethah here. You and me, kid, we don't need nobody else. Now I gotta think uh the next step. Oh yeah! Wear a black suit.

BRINKLEY

A black suit?

CLARA BOW

Well ya can't do somethin' like this wearin' a fuckin' dress 'n' angora cardigan. Have some respect, for God's sake. Ya got enough black suits. Pick one. Ya got a closet like a fuckin' funeral director.

(laughs)

A funeral director who loves angora!

BRINKLEY

That's not funny.

CLARA BOW

'Course it's funny. Ya wanna know what's funny? Look in the mirror! In this life, ya gotta take yer laughs where you can get 'em.

BRINKLEY

(hurt)

You told me once that you think I'm handsome.

CLARA BOW

(smirking and placating)

That's right, baby. You're handsome, handsome as they come.

BRINKLEY

Clara?

CLARA BOW

Yeah?

BRINKLEY

When I assemble all of these ingredients, I won't know what to do with them.

CLARA BOW

That's why ya got me. But ya gotta do the assemblin' part on yer own. I can't leave this room 'til all uh the particulars are in order and ready ta go. So come back here when you're ready.

BRINKLEY

I'm scared.

CLARA BOW

Everybody's scared, Brinkley. But ya do what ya gotta do. Don't be such a sap.

BRINKLEY

I'm sorry. You're right, you're always right. Is there anything else I need?

CLARA BOW

Yeah. Matches and a candle. A white candle. And yer Kleenex dispenser.

BRINKLEY

Thank you. I could never do this without you. Clara? May I kiss you again?

CLARA BOW

Later, baby. Right now, ya got work ta do.

II

Electronic snowstorm replaced the image of Brinkley and Clara Bow. No wonder he was in Hell with me. But then again, what kind of Divine Authority would sentence a man to the Room of Doom just because he wanted to end his mother's suffering? Well, granted, that wasn't the only reason he had apparently offed her: he wanted to pay her back for making his life miserable by being first a raving lunatic bitch and then a diseased raving lunatic bitch who moaned all night and kept him awake. And rightly so. You can't blame a man for that—can you? Don't partly pure intentions count for anything? Oh wait, what was that line about the road to Hell being paved with . . . Damn. Did that mean Clara Bow was here, too? She was, after all, an accessory. The mastermind, in fact. She goaded him into it. Maybe everyone who'd ever lived was drowning in the Styx. Maybe everyone was excluded from Heaven, because Heaven didn't exist. But if there is no goodness, does evil have a point?

I wondered if I really was psychic since I'd suggested to Brinkley that he would have been right to put a pillow over his mother's face, and such an act was now slated to be the climax of the unfolding drama. But my suggestion had been more a turn of phrase, not a premonition. And what did I care if I was psychic, because I seemed to be missing the most important prediction of all—when I was getting the hell out of Hell.

I had always thought time travel possible, and getting to know Clara Bow through my mirror was a refreshing confirmation of my suspicion.

Maybe other people couldn't see her, but that didn't mean she wasn't real. (Exhibit A: Shadowman.) The more I watched her, the more I knew she was as real as Brinkley and me. Based on what I'd read, everything she said about her life was true. So a 1920s movie star was helping him to kill his mother. Because she was brave enough to say and do all the things he couldn't, or couldn't without assistance. I wished I'd had such a supportive friend. I could see and hear Clara with perfect clarity, as Brinkley could, and admired her more every moment. The reel that was our lives threw everyone else's reel out the window.

So I faced a dilemma of sorts, because I really wanted to write to Brinkley and tell him that I admired his courage, his personal act of justice. But if I was being judged on some karmic level, maybe that would be a bad idea. Of course, I had already expressed my opinion that he should have put out his mother's lights for good, but that was before I knew he'd really done it.

Well, I hadn't seen it happen yet. And I wasn't going to write until I had.

INT. BRINKLEY'S HELL—MIRROR—
DAVIE'S APARTMENT—BEDROOM—NIGHT

Velvet sits on Davie's bed eating a falafel. Davie paces, stops short. He addresses a packed theatre.

DAVIE

"To be, or not to be: that is the question."

VELVET

Existential babble.

DAVIE

"Now is the winter of our discontent."

VELVET

(laughs)

No kidding. When are you gonna get the heat fixed in here?

DAVIE

"O, she doth teach the torches to burn bright!"

VELVET

Who was burning your torch last night?

Davie somersaults onto the bed.

DAVIE

Gimme some.

Velvet feeds him falafel.

VELVET

Witches or warlocks?

DAVIE

A witch. Who turned out to be a bitch. No warlocks in sight. Wasn't in the mood, anyway. Though they tend to be less complicated.

VELVET

Maybe you should stay away from the witches. Or bitches. Are they bitchy witches or witchy bitches?

DAVIE

No can do. If there's more than one flavour, why limit yourself?

She touches his face, wipes food from the corner of his mouth.

VELVET

Be Romeo again.

DAVIE

You're always interrupting me.

VELVET

I won't interrupt. Promise. Cross my heart and kiss my kneecap.

He rolls off the mattress and crouches, looks upward.

DAVIE

"But soft! what light through yonder window breaks?/ It is the east, and Juliet is the sun!/ Arise, fair sun, and kill the envious moon,/ Who is already sick and pale with grief,/ That thou her maid art far more fair than she:/ Be not her maid, since she is envious;/ Her vestal livery is but sick and green,/ And none but fools do wear it; cast it off./ It is my lady; O, it is my love!/ O, that she knew she were!"

Velvet stares at him as though at one risen from the dead. Her eyes are huge and shining. Davie notices her expression.

DAVIE

What's wrong?

She shrugs.

DAVIE

What is it?

Shrugs.

DAVIE

What? Is he here? The Shadowman? I won't let him hurt you, Velcro Chenille.

VELVET

I . . .

DAVIE

"She speaks:/ O, speak again, bright angel!"

VELVET

I don't know.

DAVIE

You're overwhelmed by the force of my performance? My magnetism strummed your deepest chords? And I wasn't even halfway through!

VELVET

Will you cuddle me?

DAVIE

Cuddle? Don't you have a stuffed animal for that? Fuck, Velvet, you scared me. I thought you were about to flip your wig again.

Velvet holds out her arms.

DAVIE

Jesus. Just for a minute.

He sits on the bed, holds her awkwardly.

VELVET

How come you hold other witches and not me?

DAVIE

I don't hold anyone. There is no holding going on.

VELVET

You don't fuck me, so you have to hold me.

Davie stands up, moves away.

DAVIE

I don't have to do anything.

Velvet gets off the mattress, stands before him.

VELVET

Fine. Don't do anything. Just stand still. And you don't have to tell me you love me, even though I know you do.

She places her hands on his face.

DAVIE

Are you done?

VELVET

No. And thank you.

DAVIE

For what?

VELVET

For all the times you've come to visit me at the Cracker Farm.

Davie shrugs, embarrassed, but looks at her tenderly.

DAVIE

Don't mention it. I keep hoping they'll give me some free pills.

VELVET

(smiles)

Pharmaceuticals are never the answer. They make you feel like shit.

DAVIE

Duly noted. But the Shadowman doesn't seem to float your boat either.

VELVET

True. But he gives me some good ideas. And I can always trust him to come back. Which is more than I can say for most people.

DAVIE

Are you done touching my face now?

VELVET

No.

DAVIE

How 'bout now?

VELVET

No.

He turns, pulls a takeout menu off the wall.

DAVIE

Let's order something.

VELVET

We just ate.

DAVIE

I'm still hungry.

VELVET

You're a bottomless pit.

DAVIE

Yeah. You could say that. Chinese?

VELVET

Whatever.

DAVIE

Egg rolls, wonton soup, extra fortune cookies.

VELVET

Far Eastern Providence papers.

DAVIE

Providence is easier to take in a cookie.

VELVET

You're an atheist.

DAVIE

Remember, it depends on my mood, which depends on my blood sugar. One bite of a cookie and I'm a Believer.

VELVET

You are spiritually ridiculous.

DAVIE

How do you say that in Latin? I should start a church.

VELVET

A church for the spiritually ridiculous? Run by an atheist?

DAVIE

Yeah, we'd have tons of fortune cookies and Coke, so everyone'd be praying up a storm in no time. Actually, that's not a bad idea for a play. Write me a play about a guy who's made the arcane association between insulin and God, and parlayed his findings into a church for diabetic atheists. Oh, and he delivers all of his sermons in iambic pentameter.

VELVET

Sounds like a Tony Award winner.

DAVIE

You can be my nun.

VELVET

I can't act.

DAVIE

You don't need to act. You just hafta lie down.

VELVET

Oh, so it's a porno too. Wouldn't that be a rip-off of some Catholic play?

DAVIE

What, you think the Catholics have cornered the porn market?

VELVET

Don't talk to me about writing. That goddamn novella has already consumed my sanity.

DAVIE

What sanity?

VELVET

Fuck you.

DAVIE

Ah well, when you've got one foot in the nut factory, you might as well make wrenches.

VELVET

Are you comparing my novella to a wrench?

DAVIE

But then again, shouldn't it be tightening your screws, not loosening them?

VELVET

My screws *are* tight.

DAVIE

Let me see your wrist.

VELVET

Fuck off.

DAVIE

Exhibit A. I'm just sayin'.

VELVET

Yeah, well, I'm not writing some play about a diabetic Shakespearean preacher.

DAVIE

I'm moving.

VELVET

Because I won't write the play? You write the play.

DAVIE

No, because I can't get any work.

VELVET

What are you talking about?

DAVIE

I'm moving to L.A.

VELVET

That's not funny.

DAVIE

I'm not joking. I'm sick of auditioning for shitty TV shows.

VELVET

There're shitty TV shows in L.A. too. Even more of them.

DAVIE

I don't wanna stay here.

She gazes as if down the barrel of a gun. The shiny surfaces of her eyes shift their clarities, as a cloud passes over sky.

VELVET

Say you're joking. This is a mean fucking joke. Say you're joking.

DAVIE

I'm not—

VELVET

Say it! Say it! Say you're joking!

DAVIE

I'm not joking! I'm sorry, I can't stay here anymore! I've been wanting to tell—

VELVET

How can you leave me? Who the fuck is gonna visit me at the Cracker Farm? Nobody else'll understand!

DAVIE

I'm not gonna sacrifice my life to your psychotic mess!

VELVET

Fuck you! That's what you do when you love something—you let it barf all over you! Who's gonna visit me in the Quiet Room?

DAVIE

Your mother'll visit you! Or get some new friends!

She rushes at him, pummels his chest. He shoves her across the room and she crashes into the produce crate-cum-night stand, knocking over the camera and the photographs of herself.

DAVIE

Velvet, stop it! For fuck's sake! I don't wanna live in this fucking dump! And I hate this fucking provincial little town!

Velvet is curled on the floor with her arms wrapped tight around herself, as if trying to keep warm. She begins to knock her head against the wall.

VELVET

Don't leave me. Don't leave me. Don't leave me. Don't leave me. Don't leave me.

DAVIE

Velvet, stop!

She screams, a sound that rends the vocal cords: the fatal roots of a mandrake.

VELVET

Don't! Don't! Don't! Don't! Don't!

The head-bashing increases in vigour. Davie runs to her and grabs her head.

DAVIE

Stop it! Stop!

He holds her face and she looks at him with dazed eyes, a sleepy sojourner returning on the caboose of a dream-train.

DAVIE

Jesus. You're gonna knock yourself out. Velvet!

The dazed dreamer dives off the train.

VELVET

Don't you say my name! Don't you dare say my name! You motherfucker!

A shove to the chest and a run across the room. She falls to the floor and cocoons her legs in her arms, begins to rock.

VELVET

You . . . can't . . . leave . . . me. . . . You can't!

DAVIE

You know what? Fuck you! Fuck you, fuck you, fuck you!

He starts for the door.

VELVET

Wait!

Charges after him. Flings herself at his feet, wrapping her arms around his legs.

VELVET

I'm sorry. I'm sorry. I'm sorry. I'm sorry. I'm sorry. Don't go. Don't go. Don't go. Don't go. Don't go.

Quiet, save for stifled sobs. Two players tableauing misery.

DAVIE

You have five seconds to let go of me or I promise you will be sorry.

She releases his legs, sits on the floor looking up at him.

VELVET

I don't want to be all alone. You understand me.

DAVIE

So get a boyfriend. Get a life.

A strangled cry sounds. Velvet grabs Davie's hand and bites down. He screams and smashes her across the face. She falls back and he runs into the bathroom, swearing. She touches her bloodied mouth. A shadow grows on the opposite wall.

VELVET

Davie! Davie! Davie!

The Shadowman appears in drag as a 1930s Marlene Dietrich-style German cabaret performer, singing "Good Times" from *Kiss of the Spider Woman*. He has a cigarette contained in an antique holder, and pauses his song to blow a menacing curl of smoke in Velvet's direction. Terrified, Velvet begins to crawl backward across the room.

SHADOWMAN

Vy you cry leetle gurl? What's matter? You scared? Come here, leetle gurl. Let me give you kiss. Don't you vant me to kiss you?

Velvet unlooses the shriek of burning nerves. Davie enters, and the Shadowman vanishes.

DAVIE

Fuck me. Velvet. Velvet!

She stares transfixed at the wall. Davie glances from Velvet to the wall and back again.

DAVIE

Fuck. Velvet! Hello!

He moves to her and kneels down, touches her face.

DAVIE

Hey, Vee. Look at me. Velvet.

Her eyes flicker as though changing trains in consciousness, jostled by station platform confusion. She looks at him, unseeing.

DAVIE

There's no one here, Velcro Chenille. There's no one but me.

Her stare is steady, unbroken blankness.

DAVIE

Fuck! I can't. I can't. Let's sit on the bed.

Velvet's eyes see his face, and her mouth smiles a smile that isn't sure why it smiles. They move to the bed.

DAVIE

Hi.

VELVET

Hi.

DAVIE

There's blood on your mouth. There's nobody here but me.

VELVET

Of course not. Why would you say that?

DAVIE

Vee . . .

VELVET

I know there's nobody. But he was here a second ago!

DAVIE

Okay, okay. Do you need to go to the hospital?

VELVET

Are you crazy? I'm not going back there.

(pointedly)

Who's gonna visit me?

Davie looks away for a moment, then looks at Velvet and tries to smile.

DAVIE

(pause)

That's a prizefighter's lip you got there.

She touches her mouth.

VELVET

Do I look like Rocky?

DAVIE

Kind of. You ever bite me again I'll have to kill you. Got it?

She nods.

VELVET

You're really moving to L.A.?

DAVIE

You gonna come visit me? Swim in my pool?

VELVET

You've got a pool?

DAVIE

No. But I'm sure we could find one. And I'm getting a poodle.

VELVET

A poodle?

DAVIE

I'm gonna name it Come Back Little Sheba. I'll call it Comeback for short.

VELVET

Comeback.

DAVIE

Yeah.

VELVET

Yeah.

INT. VELVET'S HELL—MIRROR—BRINKLEY'S BEDROOM—NIGHT

Brinkley stands before Clara, recipe cards and pen in hand. He is dressed in a black suit. On his bed sits a basket filled with his Cotswold cottage Kleenex dispenser, a bowl of salt, a bottle of aspirin, a wet cloth, a jar of pickles, a candle, matches, and a blue pillow.

CLARA BOW

You look real nice, baby, real nice. Where's your hearse?

She laughs hysterically.

BRINKLEY

That's not funny. You're making me very nervous. Please stop laughing.

CLARA BOW

I'm sorry. You won't hear another giggle outta me.

She snorts and dissolves into hysterics.

BRINKLEY

I mean it! Or I won't speak to you anymore!

CLARA BOW

Don't you threaten me, you little shit! You need me! You need me! Remember that. You can't do none uh this without me.

BRINKLEY

I'm sorry, Clara, I'm sorry, I'm sorry. But please don't laugh. This is not a laughing matter.

CLARA BOW

Sometimes I get the giggles, I can't help it. But they're gone now. I can cry if you want. Would that get you in the mood? Just sing "Rock-a-bye Baby."

BRINKLEY

"Rock-a-bye Baby"?

CLARA BOW

Yeah, I always ask them tuh play it for me on set. Makes me cry inna jiffy.

BRINKLEY

Why?

CLARA BOW

Makes me think uh my little friend that got burned up. His mother used ta sing it to 'im every night.

BRINKLEY

Oh. No wonder you cry. My mother never sang that song.

CLARA BOW

Neither did mine.

BRINKLEY

You look so beautiful.

CLARA BOW

Got my glad rags on. And my favourite gold heels, just fer you. They make me feel bettah. Fresh henna on my famous hair too.

BRINKLEY

You look like an angel.

CLARA BOW

Thank you. *You're* an angel. Yer ma don't deserve to have uh son so nice as you. Did you give 'er the triple scotch?

BRINKLEY

Yes.

CLARA BOW

And?

BRINKLEY

She's asleep.

CLARA BOW

Showtime!

BRINKLEY

Clara?

CLARA BOW

That's me.

BRINKLEY

I can't.

CLARA BOW

Ya can't what?

BRINKLEY

I can't do this.

CLARA BOW

Sure ya can. Ya gotta. Ya don't gotta choice in the matter. Sometimes ya gotta do what ya don't wanna. It's fer the best, baby, fer the best. Don't ya wanna be free uh her? She don't exactly make yer life a picnic. Never did. And how you evah gonna get to sleep with her drunk and cryin' all the time?

He starts to cry, and his hands shake.

CLARA BOW

Whoa, baby, careful, don't drop the cards!

Wipes his tears with recipe cards.

CLARA BOW

Honey, don't smudge the instructions. For cryin' out loud, Brinkley, pull yaself togethah. Quit bein' a sap. Jeepers creepers, you're as yella as they come. Have you done everythin' written on the cards so far?

BRINKLEY

Yes. I'm just waiting for the Chinese food to arrive.

CLARA BOW

Mmm . . . yummy. I love chop suey. You bettah write down the rest of the instructions now.

BRINKLEY

Why do I need the cards if you're coming with me?

CLARA BOW

'Cuz once we're in the room, I won't say nothin' 'til she's gone.

BRINKLEY

Why not?

CLARA BOW

'Cuz that's the way it's gotta be. Sometimes it's bettah to be quiet. So you oughta write down the rest.

BRINKLEY

All right.

(pause)

I know you are correct about all of this. I'm just so tired.

He shuffles the cards until he finds a blank one, poises his pen. His shaking is getting worse.

CLARA BOW

'Course I'm right, kid. So let's get down to business. I've never been in yer mother's room before. I'm gettin' uh little excited!

BRINKLEY

I never wanted to bring you in there. You're both redheads, and you are so beautiful, and, well, my mother, she might not like that. She is beautiful too, extremely beautiful, but—

CLARA BOW

Ya don't hafta explain it ta me. Now: whaddya need ta know?

BRINKLEY

What do I do with the blue pillow?

CLARA BOW

Whaddya mean whaddya do with it?

BRINKLEY

I mean, what do I do with it?

CLARA BOW

Brinkley. Ya wanna end yer sufferin', right? And set yaself free?

BRINKLEY

Yes.

CLARA BOW

That's what the pillow's for. You put it on her face. And ya press down. And ya wait fer five minutes. And then yer pain is ovah.

BRINKLEY

I can't do that.

CLARA BOW

Ya hafta, if ya wanna be free uh her. And if you wanna get some sleep.

BRINKLEY

I don't trust death.

CLARA BOW

Well ya sure as hell can't trust life. Does too many awful thingsta people.

BRINKLEY

That's true.

CLARA BOW

'Course it's true. She's in a dead sleep. Too bad she won't feel a thing. You'll be better off. And she'll be—well, who gives a shit?

BRINKLEY

(nodding vigorously)

Better off. Better off. Better off. Better off. Better off.

CLARA BOW

Brinkley!

BRINKLEY

Yes?

CLARA BOW

Do ya need ta write it down?

BRINKLEY

Write what down?

CLARA BOW

What tuh do with the pillow.

BRINKLEY

No. I will remember.

CLARA BOW

Good. But ya can only do the pillow thing after ya light the candle.

BRINKLEY

Candle?

CLARA BOW

Yeah. The candle. Remembah?

BRINKLEY

Oh yes! The candle! I found a candle. A white candle.

CLARA BOW

So ya light the candle, then we eat half the chop suey and a pickle, then ya sprinkle salt all around her, throw some ovah yer left shoulder, do the pillow thing and then we eat the rest uh the Chinese and read the fortunes in the cookies.

BRINKLEY

How long is the pillow thing going to take?

CLARA BOW

Five minutes. Write it down, 'cuz I won't be givin' out instructions.

Brinkley takes a deep breath and writes on a recipe card. A doorbell sounds.

BRINKLEY

(panicking)

I just heard the doorbell! The Chinese food is here!

CLARA BOW

It's showtime, kid! Don't forget, I'm yer angel.

BRINKLEY

You are a vision from Heaven.

CLARA BOW

Ya don't look half bad yaself, kid. The tie looks a damn sight better on you than the dress. Pretty handsome, I gotta say.

BRINKLEY

Thank you.

Enormous tears leak from his eyes, faucet down his face. He does not blink or move.

CLARA BOW

It's time, baby. And if ya don't quit cryin' and act like a man I'm gonna hafta kill ya. Got it? Now come on. Yer audience is waitin'.

BRINKLEY

My audience?

CLARA BOW

Yeah. Me.

BRINKLEY

I won't disappoint you, Clara.

CLARA BOW

I know, Brinkley.

BRINKLEY

I love you, Clara.

CLARA BOW

I know, Brinkley.

12

In the beginning, a glow: gone was the movie, gone was the electronic snow, and a golden glow took their place, a warm, modest, melting glow, not a blinding light (that would be cliché, though for that very reason I was surprised Hell hadn't scorched my eyeballs with the blaze of a thousand suns, and paired it with a bad pop song) and from that warmth emerged many pairs of golden hands, beckoning me into the mirror. I was too busy staring in wonderment to note my lack of fear, but maybe I did note it, in some cobwebbed corner, and took it for knowledge that I wasn't staring down the Devil's digits, and a wisp of possibility, a waif of hope (for hope had grown fashionably anorexic) that maybe God existed, and I had been remembered. The hands grew larger, reaching into the room toward me, long and elegant and lush and inviting, as though an eternal warm bath was cupped in the palms.

I dove in.

INT. RITA/MOTHER'S BEDROOM—NIGHT

Velvet glances around, looking very much like someone blinded by a light. Rita/Mother, drastically aged, is passed out on the bed. Velvet jumps as Brinkley and Clara Bow enter.

VELVET

Brinkley!

He does not hear or see her. Clara does, and she smiles and waves, then places a finger to her lips. She retreats into a corner and sits on the floor. Velvet moves to Brinkley, awe and tenderness marrying in her eyes, and touches his shoulder. He does not feel her. He moves away, places his basket and a plastic bag full of takeout cartons on a dresser, takes out the candle and packet of matches. She looks at Clara, who motions her over. Velvet remains still another moment, casting a longing glance at Brinkley, who is trying and failing to strike a match. Then she goes to the corner, sits on the floor beside the movie star. Brinkley's hands are shaking so badly his match-lighting efforts are yielding no results. Sweat dews his face. When a flame finally appears he lights the candle, then lets the match burn while he stares transfixed at the belly-dancing roll of fire until it scorches his fingers. Velvet and Clara Bow cringe. He removes a takeout carton from the plastic bag and opens it, takes out two pairs of chopsticks and slips them from their paper coverings. They make a snapping sound as he breaks them apart. He eats a bit of the chop suey, gags, chokes, recovers, and carries it and a pair of chopsticks over to Clara Bow, places both on the floor in front of her, as though making an offering at a shrine. His eyes gaze at Clara's; Velvet's eyes gaze at his. Brinkley moves back to the dresser and opens the jar of pickles, eats one. The crunch seems to soothe him. He wipes his face with the wet cloth, scrubbing hard, and pulls a Kleenex from the Cotswold cottage chimney, blows his nose. Out comes the bowl of salt: he spills a little as he crosses from the dresser to Rita/Mother's sleeping form. When he is beside her, his eyes widen and a strangled cry spazzes his throat; he backs away, then advances, retreats then advances again. Fingertip to salt, fingertip to tongue: he tastes it. Nodding, he sprinkles salt all around Rita/Mother, throws the remainder over his left shoulder. Back to the dresser, where he puts down the bowl and picks up the blue pillow. He crosses to the centre of the room, in between the dresser and the bed, and stands helpless and still, hugging the pillow. He looks at Clara, an impish smile twitching his lips. A snorting laugh unlooses. And then another. Clara begins to giggle. Velvet looks from one to the other, before letting out a snort of her own. All three shriek with laughter. Brinkley falls to the floor, clutching his stomach. Clara gasps for air while attempting to put a finger to her lips.

Velvet can't stop snorting, which makes her laugh even harder. Brinkley picks himself up and staggers to the bed, still wracked by spasms of laughter. He muffles his mouth with his hands. Then, in a sudden burst of motion, he grabs the pillow and plunges it down. Rita/Mother's body jerks and writhes, a mad spider. While he presses the pillow he counts, softly. Clara Bow continues to giggle, poking Velvet and pointing at the bed. Velvet watches with eyes huge and blinkless. Rita/Mother's body stops moving, but Brinkley counts on. When Brinkley has counted five sets of sixty, he backs away from the body and falls into a rocking chair. He looks at Clara as if waiting for further instructions. She attempts to compose herself, stands and mimes rocking a baby.

CLARA BOW

(sings)

"Rock-a-bye, baby
In the treetop
When the wind blows
The cradle will rock . . .
When the bough breaks
The cradle will fall
And down will come baby
Cradle and all . . ."

Clara curtsies. Brinkley claps, as though at an opera. Both begin to laugh again, and soon they are helpless, Brinkley on the chair, Clara on the floor. Velvet rushes to him, kneels and clasps his hand. He does not notice her.

VELVET

Brinkley! Brinkley, it's me, Velvet! I'm here!

He shrieks with mirth and his convulsions infect Velvet, who holds his hand and cries with laughter. Clara dances around the room.

CLARA BOW

Ding dong, the witch is dead!

Brinkley's laughter subsides. Now he has the hiccups, and Velvet catches them.

CLARA BOW

Drink from the wrong side uh the cup, that's the ticket. Gets ridda them in a jiffy. Or do ya have a sugar cube? Put one on yer tongue and plug yer nose.

BRINKLEY

No.

(hiccup)

Hold your

(hiccup)

breath for ten seconds.

He takes a deep breath, puffing out his cheeks. Velvet follows suit.

BRINKLEY

See? All better. Works every time.

CLARA BOW

Yer ma's all better too! Better dead!

Clara laughs and Brinkley nods. She twirls around, swinging her arms.

CLARA BOW

Good show, baby, good show!

BRINKLEY

Aspirin time?

CLARA BOW

Absolutely!

BRINKLEY

How many?

CLARA BOW

Nine.

VELVET

Nine? That's too many!

Brinkley can't hear her and Clara ignores her. Velvet starts toward Brinkley, but Clara glares at her and she stops. Brinkley swallows the pills one at a time, without water, chewing a little. He pulls a Kleenex from the Cotswold chimney and wipes sweat from his face, rubs the wet cloth over the front and back of his neck, inside his ears.

CLARA BOW

Time for Chinese food, baby. We gotta send yer ma off right. She got what was comin' to 'er. And now you're free!

Brinkley nods. He moves to a small vanity table next to the rocking chair, where a mirror hangs, and picks up a gold tube of red lipstick, takes off the cap and turns it up all the way. He draws a heart on the mirror, framing his reflection, and poses. He mimes holding a microphone, and sings "My Funny Valentine."

Clara claps wildly and Brinkley bows. He returns to the dresser, picks up the plastic bag, drops to the floor and begins unpacking the Chinese food.

BRINKLEY

Dinnertime.

Clara is doing the Charleston.

CLARA BOW

A little party, in honour uh you finally havin' the guts!

BRINKLEY

You're a great dancer.

CLARA BOW

Dancin' is Heaven!

BRINKLEY

Do you believe in Hell, Clara?

CLARA BOW

(still dancing)

You'll never go there, that's fer sure!

BRINKLEY

What about my mother?

Clara stops dancing.

CLARA BOW

That's not fer you ta decide, baby. Ya did the right thing. Cross my heart 'n' kiss my earlobes. Let's eat I'm starvin'!

Velvet sits with Brinkley and Clara on the floor, watching as they devour the Chinese takeout.

CLARA BOW

Hello. Sorry I didn't introduce myself earlier. I hadda keep my mouth shut 'til he did the pillow thing. My name's Clara Bow.

She extends her hand to Velvet, who shakes it.

VELVET

Yes, I know who you are. The great movie star. The "It Girl" of the '20s. It's an honour to meet you.

Brinkley is unaware of their conversation.

CLARA BOW

Ah well, thanks. The movie business is murder, I can tell ya that much.

VELVET

I'm sure it is. You're so beautiful. Um . . . How is it that you're here?

CLARA BOW

Whaddya mean?

VELVET

I mean, how can you be here? Do you time travel?

CLARA BOW

How could I be anywhere else? I'm Brinkley's special friend.

VELVET

So am I.

CLARA BOW

So that's why you're here?

VELVET

Yeah. That's why I'm here. But he can't see me.

CLARA BOW

What can I say, honey? He's only got eyes fer me.

(pause)

Sorry fer askin', but do you got uh disease or somethin'? How come yer hair is different colors? And you got bald patches. How come yer eyes look kinda funny?

VELVET

Um, no, I don't have a disease. It's a long story.

(pause)

Will you tell him sometime that I was here?

CLARA BOW

Sure I will. What's yer name?

VELVET

Velvet.

CLARA BOW

Yer name's Velvet? That's the bee's knees! I love velvet opera coats.

VELVET

Thanks. So do I.

Clara pulls open the bag of fortune cookies. She cracks a cookie.

CLARA BOW

(reads)

"You have the qualities to become a star."

(throws it over her shoulder and snorts)

Ha! Tell me somethin' I don't know.

She cracks another cookie.

CLARA BOW

(reads)

"You will live a very happy life."

(rips it up)

Bullshit! This stuff's bunk! Read yours, Brinkley.

BRINKLEY

(cracks one and reads)

"You will find true love where you least expect it."

Clara giggles and looks coy.

BRINKLEY

I love you, Clara.

CLARA BOW

That's right, baby.

Velvet looks long at Brinkley. She reaches out and touches his face.

VELVET

(softly)

Brinkley . . .

CLARA BOW

Brinkley! Watch this!

She jumps up and runs across the room, begins to Charleston wildly beside Rita/Mother's body. Brinkley forces a smile.

BRINKLEY

You're a real floorflusher.

Velvet places both her hands on his face. She touches his hair.

VELVET

(softly)

Brinkley, I want you to know that I—

The pink-walled menace, my bedroom Hell, closed in around me tight as a fat fist as I sat, once again, in the middle of the carpet.

INT. DAVIE'S APARTMENT—LIVING ROOM—NIGHT

Brinkley looks around, startled at where he finds himself. The apartment is in boxes and Velvet sits on one by the window, her eyes at sea in the night. She wears a red velvet mandarin-collared dress, jewel-encrusted high-heeled sandals, a cloche hat and black lace gloves. Her make-up is artful and dramatic: Egyptianesque kohl-lined eyes and red lips. Davie paces, fiddling with his camera.

BRINKLEY

Velvet!

She does not hear or see him, and neither does Davie.

BRINKLEY

Velvet!

He moves to her, touches her shoulder.

BRINKLEY

Velvet, it's me.

She does not feel him.

VELVET

(looking at Davie)

I don't feel like having my picture taken.

DAVIE

What are you talking about? You always want me to take your picture.

VELVET

Not now.

DAVIE

This is our window shot. One last time before I go.

She returns her eyes to the night beyond the window.

VELVET

Don't say that.

(pause)
Do your Groucho Marx.

DAVIE

(as Groucho)
"You're heading for a breakdown, why don't you pull yourself to pieces?" "Either this man is dead or my watch has stopped."

Velvet smiles.

VELVET

More!

DAVIE

(as Groucho)
"Go, and never darken my towels again."

She laughs.

VELVET

You're better than the real Groucho Marx.

Brinkley crouches at Velvet's feet, his hand resting on top of hers. He never takes his eyes off her.

VELVET

There any egg rolls left in your fridge?

DAVIE

Yeah. A couple.

She gets up and moves to the kitchen. Brinkley follows her, still holding her hand.

INT. DAVIE'S APARTMENT—KITCHEN—CONTINUOUS

Velvet, unaware, pulls her hand away from his when she opens the refrigerator, but he continues to stand very close.

From the fridge she pulls a squashed carton, opens it and forces an entire egg roll into her mouth with the heel of her hand, then leans against the door, trying to chew. Brinkley picks up a homemade, real-potato Mr. Potato Head, who wears tiny pipe cleaner glasses and a red- and blue-striped tie. He picks up another, who wears a little satin evening dress cut on the bias. He fingers the material.

DAVIE

(O.S.)

Maybe I should go to New York instead. I wanna be in *Kiss of the Spider Woman*.

VELVET

(mouth full)

Its Broadway run closed a zillion years ago. Besides, you can't sing.

DAVIE

(O.S.)

Fuck off.

Davie sings "Anything For Him" from *Kiss of the Spider Woman*, his voice off-key. Velvet stuffs another egg roll in her mouth, chokes. Brinkley rubs her back.

BRINKLEY

(softly)

Velvet, look at me.

DAVIE

(O.S.)

You finished in there, Miss Piggy?

VELVET

Fuck you.

DAVIE

(O.S.)

Ooh, testy.

Davie sticks his head in the kitchen.

DAVIE

Come on, Velcro Chenille. Picture's up.

Brinkley stares at Davie, shakes his head.

VELVET

All right, coming.

INT. DAVIE'S APARTMENT—LIVING ROOM—CONTINUOUS

VELVET

Where should I stand?

Brinkley stands next to Velvet.

DAVIE

By the window.

Brinkley follows Velvet to the window, then darts into a corner when Davie points the camera in their direction. Velvet looks out at the sky.

VELVET

Full moon.

DAVIE

No wonder I've got cramps.

VELVET

PMS?

DAVIE

Full moons wreak havoc with my hormones, darling. Now, look straight at me. Fabulous hat, darling, fabulous hat. *Trés* Golden Age of Hollywood.

VELVET

Are you going to hang these pictures in your new apartment?

DAVIE

But of course, my dear. If they turn out. Okay, stand still. Don't smile.

VELVET

Don't worry. I won't.

Davie begins snapping photos. Velvet's doleful stare is steadfast and unblinking.

DAVIE

Relax. You look like a zombie mannequin.

VELVET

Maybe I should come to L.A. with you.

DAVIE

What would you do in L.A.?

VELVET

I don't know. Handle your costumes.

DAVIE

They have studio people for that. Suck in your stomach. The egg rolls aren't flattering the dress.

BRINKLEY

(softly, from the corner)

She's beautiful, just as she is.

VELVET

Maybe we should each get one of those picture frames that record a voice message, so you can have a picture of me and a bit of my voice, and I can have a picture of you and a bit of your voice. But I know we'll be talking on the phone.

Davie snaps away.

DAVIE

Tilt your chin up and to the left.

VELVET

Stop shooting.

He continues.

VELVET

Stop . . . Stop!

He lowers the camera.

DAVIE

What?

VELVET

Won't you miss me?

He looks away.

VELVET

Davie. I'll miss you.

DAVIE

Sure. Sure I'll miss you, Velcro Chenille. You know I will.

(straining for humour)

I won't have anyone to visit in the psych ward!

(pause)

I . . . love you. You know that?

VELVET

(softly)

Stay. Please stay. For me.

Davie looks at her. Neither blinks. Moments pass. Velvet pulls off her gloves, finger by finger. She undoes her dress, steps out of it. She is not wearing undergarments. She kicks off her sandals. From his corner, Brinkley watches, drop-jawed. Velvet moves toward Davie, wearing only her cloche hat. A marmoreal mask of almost-fear has settled over his features. When she reaches him, she removes the camera from his hand and sets it on the floor. He opens his mouth to speak, but she covers it with her hand. She touches his cheek, places his hand on her breast. Davie looks like a small, lost boy, terrified into stillness. Velvet backs him into a chair, pulls off his shirt, then his pants. He does not resist, nor does he help. Brinkley remains in the corner. Velvet lowers herself into Davie's lap. He does not touch her, but sits straight and rigid in the chair, as on a throne: "The Emperor's No Clothes." She covers his eyes, places her mouth on his. Brinkley sits on the floor in a tight rocking ball, his face half-buried in his arms. His strange eyes glow like limelight, trained in unbroken beams on the couple in the chair. Velvet and Davie kiss for a moment, awkwardly; he is still not touching her. She bites down hard on his lip; he cries out and shoves her, but she hangs on and they fall to the floor. A heap of tangled, wrestling limbs, mouths that snarl and bite. Both Velvet and Davie's lips are bloody. She pierces his ear with her teeth, he digs his teeth and nails into her shoulders. A victor with a mount: Velvet is on top, Davie is inside her. The Shadowman appears as Zorro. He points his rapier at Velvet.

SHADOWMAN

Whore! Whore! Whore! Whore! Whore!

Velvet shrieks. Brinkley gapes, shock and horror waging stiff competition for control of his face. In an instant, the Shadowman morphs, becoming the white-faced devil with long black nails. He moves at an oozing pace toward Velvet, his feet turned balletically outward, sleek as a wet panther.

SHADOWMAN

(hissing)

S-s-slut. S-s-slut. S-s-slut. S-s-slut. S-s-slut.

Velvet screams, rolls off Davie and crawls to the wall, curls up, clings to it.

DAVIE

What the—

SHADOWMAN

(advancing)

You fucking whore! Stand up, little girl. I have something to show you.

Velvet squeezes shut her eyes, plugs her ears, screams and screams. Brinkley trembles. Davie is shaking Velvet. She opens her eyes, tries to fight him off.

DAVIE

Velvet! Velvet! Velvet!

Velvet shrieks, punches him in the nose. Davie reels backward, holding his face. Velvet continues to scream.

SHADOWMAN

You little slut! You dirty little slut!

He clicks his pointed fingernails. Davie pulls on his clothes and runs from the apartment, holding his nose. Velvet covers her head with her hands. The Shadowman grabs her chin. Brinkley takes a deep breath.

SHADOWMAN

Do you want to die, little girl? Do you want to die? Would that be fun? Shall I kill you? Ooh, now that would be fun! How shall I do it? Shall I skin you alive?

VELVET

P-p-please l-leave m-m-me a-l-l-one. P-pleas-se . . .

Brinkley tears from his corner like a freed bat, grabs the Shadowman's arm and jerks him away from Velvet. The Shadowman turns in surprise.

SHADOWMAN

Who the fuck are you?

BRINKLEY

I'm her friend.

SHADOWMAN

She doesn't have any friends.

(staring at Brinkley's streaky, falling-out hair and strange, glowing eyes)

What kind of freak are you?

Velvet still crouches against the wall, covering her head. She cries softly. The Shadowman backs Brinkley toward the opposite wall.

SHADOWMAN

Shall I kill you, too?

He clicks his fingernails. Brinkley shakes. The Shadowman grabs him by the collar.

BRINKLEY

Y-you g-get out-t of h-h-here. L-leave us a-a-l-lone.

SHADOWMAN

What was that? Couldn't quite understand you, my boy. Do you speak English?

Brinkley winds up and punches the Shadowman in the jaw. The white-faced devil hits the floor, lies there in a theatrical heap. Brinkley is stunned, and looks from his fist to the Shadowman and back again. The devil staggers to his feet, holding his jaw. He shoots Brinkley a hurt, almost pouty look as he moves away.

BRINKLEY

You leave her alone! Don't ever come back!

SHADOWMAN

Oh trust me, my boy, I will be back. I will be back.

The Shadowman disappears. Brinkley looks across the room at Velvet. She remains curled against the wall, hands covering her head, eyes squeezed shut. He goes to her, drops to the floor, puts his arms around her naked body.

BRINKLEY

(softly)

He's gone now. He can't hurt you. Open your eyes.

Velvet opens her eyes, casts furtive, terrified glances around the empty room. She lowers her hands. Brinkley wipes the tears from her face.

BRINKLEY

Please look at me. Please see me.

She stares in confusion at the empty room. He places a hand on her heart.

She looks right at him, but does not see him. He touches her face.

BRINKLEY

Velvet, I want you to know that I—

13

Dear Brinkley,

I was with you when you killed your mother. You couldn't see me or feel me, but I was there. I stepped into my mirror and into your life. I watched you kill her. And then you started to laugh, and I did too—it was infectious. Sometimes murder leads to hiccups. But it wasn't murder, not really. You did the right thing. I met Clara Bow, the great movie star. I can understand why you loved her. Well, sort of. She's a spitfire, that one. So time travel must exist. That's kind of exciting. Too bad I had to come all this way to find that out.

I'm glad I got to touch you, just once. This place has its privileges.

Sincerely, Velvet

Dear Velvet,

You were the last person to touch me. The morning after I killed my mother, I was hit by a car. I am not sure what I would have done with her body—Clara hadn't given me instructions about that, and I had gone to bed worried about it.

I saw you, I spoke to you, I held you. I stepped into my mirror and there you were. Your friend Davie was not careful with you. Your love for him was the most valuable thing he had. People should always be careful with each other.

I don't think you have to worry about the Shadowman anymore. I had a bit of a showdown with him, and sent him into retreat. First punch I've ever thrown! At first he was a Zorro look-alike, cruel and taunting. Then he became the white-faced ghoul, the devil with long black nails. He came after you and you were screaming, of course you were, and so I punched him. He fell to the floor! When I told him to leave you alone, he disappeared. You looked at me, Velvet, you looked but you did not see me. What I would give to have you look me in the face, and see.

Yours very truly,
Brinkley

Dear Brinkley,

So you beat down the demon that stalked me! Thank you for protecting me. I hope you punched hard! Maybe the Shadowman is gone for good. And I have you to thank.

Davie was never careful about anything, or anyone. But he was loyal to me, and loved me in his way. I used to love it when he'd photograph me. At his best, he'd make me feel like a movie star, at his worst, well, you know . . .

I'm running out of paper. I still have some left, but so far it doesn't seem to be magically self-replacing and so I've realized that I don't have the freedom to blab. This must also be true of you. Unless you have extra legal pads, which I doubt. If you do, push some pages through. New development: voices. Can you hear them? They hurt my ears after the treacle-thick silence. I'm not sure yet what I'm listening to. A buzzing, a high-pitched beeping, a rustling. Comes in and out, like sounds from a damaged radio.

Sincerely, Velvet

Dear Velvet,

No paper to send you. I also must prune my thoughts. I heard a voice—female. Almost sounded like she was calling my name. Not sure. I shook all over. Fingers keep bleeding because I've chewed the nails down to the quick. Something worse: I saw my mother's face in the mirror. I am curled up in a corner as I write this, afraid to go near the glass. I will stare at the whiteness outside the window while I await your reply. The mirror side of the room feels haunted.

I can feel the cold needles in my spine. She always hated me. Why did I bother trying to love her?

Yours very truly,

Brinkley

Dear Brinkley,

Write smaller. You're using up too much paper. What are we going to do when it's gone? Tried shouting through the grate again, and the silence nearly killed me. (Bad pun.) Don't be afraid of your mother. She can't hurt you. You sent her packing. (Though given what I know of her, I suspect she's in the basement of this place.) Think of me. I'm holding you in my mind.

Sincerely, Velvet

P.S. My hair, what's left of it, has become a shock of white-blonde. Acceleration.

Dear Velvet,

My second-to-last remaining clump of blond hair came out in my hands! Growing older, growing younger? Perhaps the transformation of our physical bodies is a safe passage, a Get-Out-of-Jail-Free card. (I always did love Monopoly.) What becomes of the finite mind in an infinite place? Oh so many questions—the agonized dialectic of life pales in comparison to the agonized dialectic of death. Are we matter? I feel like matter, I bleed like matter. Does matter matter? (Hell does not dampen a taste for puns.)

My mother's face is still in the fucking mirror! (Pardon me.)

Yours very truly,

Brinkley

A rag doll with its stuffing knocked out—a pale-faced Raggedy Ann in the mirror. I looked smaller even than the last time I'd looked at my whittled figure. Features shifted, bones softened, custard face. I lifted my dress: smooth, tender, unadorned.

Dear Brinkley,
I loved Monopoly too. From the gangplank of Hell to the Boardwalk of reincarnation? I was a blonde baby. Are we travelling—back into the womb? A womb would beat this place by a mile.
Sincerely, Velvet

Dear Velvet,
I was a blond baby too. If there is such a thing as reincarnation, I pray I get a better womb.
Yours very truly,
Brinkley

Dear Brinkley,
I am in my mirror—my hanging self. What a horrible sight.
Velvet
P.S. Heard sirens.

Dear Velvet,
Help me. My mirror is bleeding.
B

Bleeding? His mirror was bleeding? Were we trapped in *The Shining* now?

I curved like a comma on the eyelet spread, Paddington making us into a semi-colon by sitting just above my head. The excoriating sight of my hanging self dangled in my mind. Was this the beginning of Brinkley's Judgment? Was I for some unknown reason being spared? Never a glutton for optimism, I was sure that couldn't be it. Face it, Velvet, you're next.

Rolled onto my back. Helplessness, the precursor to despair, leadened me. The note that I had pushed through the grate in a panic, telling him that my mirror wasn't bloody, it was all in his head, pinch hard and shake yourself, would be no comfort to him, I knew. I couldn't help him. He couldn't help me. We couldn't help each other.

Seemed like a much longer while had passed than usual and still no note. I stood at the desk flipping through the dwindling pages of my legal pad, doing everything I could to avoid looking at my dishrag hanging body in the mirror. This pause in the letter-flow was alarming, alarm unmitigated by deep breathing. Brinkley reeled around my mind, flung from wall to wall by a pair of bloody claws extending out of his mirror.

Velvet,

My mother is in the mirror, crying blood. Wait—now she is gone. Now the room is reflected as before. I apologize for the shaky, chicken-scratch handwriting. I am curled on the floor in the corner. In the centre of the room, there are three spots of vomit—I could not seem to keep it all in one place.

B

Voices in the room: *How is she? . . . Lift her leg . . . Do you want to do your Jane Fonda today? . . . Grab her leg, let's get the blood flowing . . .*

Blurred, as though travelling through the deep heat of a dark place. Then silence, returning like water reestablishing its mirror over the sand.

V: Did you hear the voices? Difficult to make out, but they sounded female. I'm under the sheets as I write this, heart still pounding. It was like the lid flipped off the silence and a bunch of Mexican hat dancers jumped out. Now my ears hurt, and I'm not sure whether it's from hearing the timbre of voices after so long or the density of the silence that replaced them. Mother in the mirror?

B: No voices, but a sound like a bowl hitting the floor and rolling. My skin must be getting loose—I have jumped in and out of it so many times. Yes, she is in the mirror, holding up her hands now—they are crying blood also. I want to hang my suit jacket over the glass, but I am afraid to get close to it, afraid she might reach through and grab me, or that some other terrible thing will happen. Would it matter now? What could be worse? But I believe we have asked that question before, and we have been duly and thoroughly answered. And Velvet, I really am frozen with fear—I cannot go near it. I am mostly staying under the bed, receiving your notes and writing you back. But sometimes I crave bright light, and every time I stick my head out from under the bed I am compelled to stare at the glass. I know that you see goodness in me, and for that I am so thankful, but perhaps the mirror is the truth. I am a murderer, after all.

Alfalfa. That was the only word to describe the remaining sprouts of white-blonde hair that dotted my skull. Interesting it was, to see one's skull for the first time, the shape and texture of it, its secret marks and bulges. I noted an infant's pliability, a delicate doughiness.

Though my lack of hair may have made them more striking, there could be no doubt: my eyes were huge, much bigger than any drugstore kohl pencil had ever made them appear. It was as if the rims were drawing back, and the other-planetary aquarium-blue was ever more revealed. I was becoming E.T.

The voices had stopped, but bursts of static now and then displaced the quietness, jolting me and reminding me of the times Davie and I had sat at the beach at night, in his falling-apart car, watching the moon disturb the tide and listening to music on his terrible radio. The static in the room sounded just like that radio, but it didn't come with any songs.

I crawled under the bed and pressed my hand to the grate.

V: You're not a murderer, get that through your bald head. You put her out of her misery, which is more than I would have done, and sent her off right with chow mein and fortune cookies. Will you press your hand to the grate? My hand is here, and I want us to be palm to palm, as it were, for a moment.

B: I am right here, and because I can see you so clearly in my mind, I can feel you. There are coloured lights outside my window.

V: I don't have any lights. What colours?

B: Every colour. And some—I do not think I can name them.

V: You've never seen them before?

B: They are impossible to describe. It is every colour we have known, and others we have not, all swirling together. A sight that makes a regular sunset wan by compare.

V: A sunset on acid.

B: So beautiful it hurts.

V: I'm not beautiful. The oldest infant I've ever seen, or the youngest old person. Bald, an alien.

B: So am I, and shrunken. Clara would be horrified at the sight of me.

V: I think I look kind of interesting and probably so do you. Frightening, but interesting.

B: I have the sense that we are dissolving. Perhaps I will join the colours outside.

V: Don't leave me.

B: I won't.

V: Promise me.

B: I promise.

V: I am a selfish woman.

B: You're not selfish. Who wants to be alone? I was mostly alone, but I had Clara, and she was enough for me. Alone with Clara Bow, I am okay.

V: I wish I'd met you back in life. You get me. You know how terrifying the Shadowman is. I wouldn't have been lonely if I'd known you.

B: If the Shadowman comes back, tell him I will break his face.

V: I will. That's comforting.

B: I feel brave, all of a sudden. What a nice feeling.

V: I should've been braver. Maybe if the Shadowman comes back, I will be.

B: I am certain of it.

V: How kind of you to say.

B: You are most welcome.

Lying under the bed, I ran a hand over my head. The last sprouted-grain tufts of hair came off, floated down onto the carpet. It was easier to experience such a thing in the relative dark. Skull so smooth, a warm orb under my hand. My arms and legs were satiny too, and I thought of the hundred dollars I had saved, back in my other life, hidden in the top drawer of my writing desk, to be allocated to my laser hair removal fund.

Voices fluttered in and out of the room, moths that flitted off as soon as you could almost understand them. Females mostly, but sometimes a male. The same male, I suspected.

Angels crossed my mind, but then I realized that if this was Hell they were automatically out of the picture. And, anyway, none of the sound clips I had managed to decipher lately—*blood, eat, colour, pressure*—resonated much like I imagined celestial-speak would. And angels ought to unlock the damn door and come inside, not stand in the ether sending coded messages.

I felt safer under the bed than in any other part of the room, a child in body, drawn up in a fetal curve. Pieces of torn paper were spread around me like large, dry snowflakes. Face to the grate, Tiny Tim outside a toy store.

V: So do you still think we're in the process of being reincarnated?

B: I do hope we look this terrible for a good reason.

V: I don't mean you return as a goat or some species of insect.

B: I know. Unless the Buddhists are correct. In which case I am about to sprout a tail. I hope we meet. And I hope I see Clara again. I miss her.

V: Maybe you'll make new friends that aren't time travellers. You deserve to have lots of friends.

B: So do you. But I think that we are different from other people. Which makes it hard to have lots of friends.

V: But maybe next time we would fit in. Do we really want to be dropped off—back into life?

B: Of course. That is an endless—omnipresent—hunger.

V: Why—God is a recidivist?

B: We are.

V: Yes. And now we're here.

B: God must hate me. I hate me. My mother hated me. The only person who loved me was Clara Bow.

V: And now me! No God I could ever know is capable of hating you. And while I have not been blessed with any sign of hope—except for your letters, which, when I think of it, should be enough—the same can't be said of you. The colours at your window—a surprise hope.

B: True.

V: I'm still waiting for my damn colours. Desperately trying to conjure Rainbow Brite.

B: When will I be taken back to where I came from, in the beginning?

V: You promised not to leave me.

B: We will go together.

V: What about your mother in the mirror? Illusion?

B: I am hoping so.

V: You think this is temporary, then? A waiting room.

B: Perhaps. A man of mercurial moods, am I.

V: If you had lived, what would you have done?

B: I don't understand.

V: What would you have done with your life?

B: I always wanted to go to Coney Island. Clara Bow worked at a hot dog stand there when she was a teenager.

V: Anything else?

B: I would have liked to run a little shop, in truth. A shop that sold movie memorabilia, and household items with a cinematic twist. *Nosferatu* lunchboxes, *The Sheik* hairdryers, *Casablanca* place mats. Of course, my favourite item would have been the *Children of Divorce* mouse pad, a tribute to Clara. But Clara does not compare to you. I admire you, Velvet.

V: You admire a suicide?

B: No, I admire you. You are very brave. The Shadowman is terrifying.

V: Thanks. But I'm still a suicide. He got me in the end.

B: Some cultures consider suicide a noble act.

V: You are better than I, Brinkley. What I did was not an act of love.

B: Not better, the same. What I did was not an act of love either. I did not really want to set my mother free, I wanted to set myself free.

V: We all need someone to get lost with, right? And a roadside attraction at which to ask for directions. Maybe you're that person for me.

B: You're that person for me too.

V: Wouldn't all this make an amazing novel?

B: 'Twould put my Harlequin romance to shame.

A volley of voices broke through the static.

V: Can you hear that?

B: I hear the sound of a lawnmower. And someone is reading. Dostoevsky, I think.

V: I heard: "Don't forget to wash her feet." And: "What a beautiful day!" I miss the sound of lawnmowers.

B: They're reading *Crime and Punishment*. A Judgment on me?

V: Then the Judgment will be for us both.

B: Could our mirrors be oracles? If so, then is your life my future? Please let it be so, not my mother's angry face.

V: Yes, oracles of the past—modern Greek tragedy, sans poetry, and with some lovely costumes. We're in *The Delphi Room*.

B: Most definitely someone is reading from *Crime and Punishment*. A woman. She does not sound threatening. But under such circumstances—could be taken as last rites before eternal flames.

V: If we were going to be flambéed, it would've happened already. There will be no forever of flames. You're stuck with me forever.

B: Good. That makes me believe in a God . . .

V: That is the most romantic thing anyone has ever expressed to me. Not that I deserve it, in all my flawed glory.

B: I love your flaws. The outtakes are always the best part of the movie.

V: Nothing like a good blooper reel.

B: People should give what they most need.

V: Were you an undiscovered cinephile saint, hidden on a Toronto porch?

B: No saints here. Only the scars from a mother who looked like a movie star, and a love who actually is a movie star. But everything falls away except pain and a few truths.

V: This place has made me less interested in philosophy.

B: I don't think more punishment awaits us. I am suddenly feeling quite sure of that.

V: I think we'd both fallen for a cartoon concept of Hell. What makes you so sure we're out of the woods?

B: I crawled out from under my bed to look out my window and all white is gone. Colours everywhere—liquid flowers, gossamer stars, an explosion of sunset.

V: Panic—I have no colours. All white.

B: I have a strange feeling—just below my bellybutton. Not an itch, not a tingle, not a rumble, not a ripple—but all of those.

V: A good feeling? Sounds like the beginning of an orgasm. Where's mine? (Even in this place, I'm still asking that same question.)

B: Yes, good, quite faint, like the kernel of something warm.

V: See—if those colours are a preview, you will be welcomed.

B: Welcomed where? True, I never imagined Hell would resemble the aurora borealis, but—

V: There is no denying it. Something is happening in your room. Something good. Nothing is happening in mine, save for my gruesome double in the mirror.

B: I have already said that I will not leave you. We both know that I have no power to keep that promise, but I have all the power necessary to mean it.

I always wondered if our dreams were our real existence, enclosed in a real world, and the lives we remember, the people, the jobs, the hours, were only the black wraith of that, a waiting in line to get back inside.

V: If truth is so subject to interpretation, what is the difference between truth and a lie? Intention, I suppose. Things, important things, must happen of which you have no memory, while some of the mind's clear photographs of events must in fact be spectres of wishful thinking, or suggestion.

B: One thing is for certain: there is no clear divide between fact and fiction, reality and memory, event and imagination. Clara told me that once. The smell of vomit is making me sick all over again. I left my hiding spot under the bed and searched for some disinfectant, wet wipes, etc. No luck. Laughable, I suppose. Why do we do things we know will be fruitless? My reward: I vomited again. My mother is there, the eye of all, an endless stream of bloody tears. Funny that I can throw up, since it was a lifetime ago that I ate something. The nature of: I suppose we can regurgitate *ad infinitum*. The feeling in my stomach is getting stronger—if I go, you know everything. The sound of *Crime and Punishment* is soothing to me. The woman's voice is sweet. She draws out the words as though she likes the feel of them in her mouth. Quieter now. Some of the words I am losing.

V: Say nothing of leaving. Don't mention it again.

Voices still buzzed in my room, low and hazy, like flies drunk on summer. No one reading literature, though. I rolled half out from under the bed, as if maybe it was the dust ruffle that separated me from *Crime and Punishment*. Nothing. Wriggled right out into the open, awaited the aural Dostoevsky bullet. Words ordinary filled the room: *good weather, traffic, coffee, lunch.* None meshed and contorted to form a Russian's literary zenith. An odd flare lit my stomach, sent tingles of tightness into my chest. Inventory: glad, mad, sad? No: jealous. Because my neighbour in *The Delphi Room*, or who-knows-where, gets to listen to a literary classic and I don't. I started laughing and couldn't stop. Until: a voice clear and strong filled the room.

Dr. Bell to Cardiology, please, Dr. Bell to Cardiology.

I made no abrupt movement of surprise. Rather the floor seemed to give way, taking several of my internal organs with it. I lay very still, the moment that held the voice running up ahead of me, my mind with its two left feet staggering to catch up.

And then—

Velvet. Velvet, come back to me.

My mother. My mother. My mother. My mother. My mother. My mother.

Now I sat up. I could see the knife, slicing three words into the skin of my mind:

WE'RE NOT DEAD

V: We're not dead!!!

B: What?

V: I just heard my mother's voice as clear as if she was standing in my room. And she is—my hospital room! Right before she spoke I heard someone paging a Dr. Bell to Cardiology. We're alive! We're not trapped in Hell—we're trapped in a coma!

B: Are you sure? Hallucination?

V: We're alive!!! I'm not hallucinating. I know my mother's voice. She was calling me back to her—loud and clear. And the doctor. Why would I hallucinate a doctor being paged? All of the voices and sounds we've heard—hospital noise. *Crime and Punishment* is not a precursor to Hellfire—someone is reading to you at your bedside. We will see each other after all—we just have to wake up! When I do, I'll take the train. I'll come to Toronto and find you. We're only trapped in our minds.

B: If we are trapped in our minds, then how is it that we can write to each other?

V: The body is a trap—but I guess the spirit can travel. Just like Clara can time travel.

B: How do we wake up? We've thrown ourselves against walls, screamed, cried. What next?

V: I don't know. Hold on—I'm going to try the door again.

An unrecorded feat of record-breaking speed—out from under the bed to the door, my heart gorging on blood. Then—a scene from the past unfolded again: me yanking on the doorknob, twisting the skin on my hands in all directions, sliding down the door still clutching the knob, the bilious taste of disappointment stinging my tongue.

V: Door's still locked. But if we're trapped in our minds then it stands to reason that we can think our way out of this! Since we exist in a state of timelessness (read: coma) then the past, present and future are one. The future already exists, has already passed—we're already free! We must believe this, and it'll happen.

B: Our thoughts are that powerful?

V: Yes—all thought must manifest somewhere, right? Thoughts are nonperishable items, like canned foods or Kraft Dinner.

B: I dislike Kraft Dinner.

V: Fuck, you're missing the point.

B: Sorry.

V: We have to focus!

B: I am trying, but the exquisite colours at my window are distracting me.

V: Forget about the damn rainbow for a minute. We've got to think our way out of here.

B: If you are correct, then we're in Hell because we believed it was so? If thoughts are things, dreams—and nightmares—can be realities. How do we keep our thought-forms from eating us? The creation kills the artist?

V: Yes, we are in a Hell—of sorts. Which can exist anywhere. But the fiery Hell we were afraid of must simply be a garbage dump of imaginings. So we're bound only by a coma—not by any red-deviled daydreams. There must be a way we can untwist our wires.

B: The colours outside my window are more dazzling than ever. They pulse and vibrate—they are living, breathing hearts—sublime, shimmering wings. We don't speak a language that could ever express what I see. Something is happening to me—a spiral tube has appeared, a tube with many twisting offshoots, superimposed over the colours like a strange, diaphanous flower. All voices are gone.

V: If you concentrate maybe you can erase all that. We can think ourselves free!

B: Impossible to erase it. And I don't want to. I can't turn away.

V: What are you saying?

B: I have no power to decide my fate.

V: Please don't go. Return to Toronto. Let me find you!

B: I am not going back to my old life. So this is what it feels like to die. Happy.

V: I want to die too. But for a different reason than before.

V: Brinkley?

V: Brinkley—answer me!

Hand to the grate, felt for a poke of paper. A blast of cold air, real or imagined, ordered up a side of goosebumps. Into the light, faced my mirror. There I hung. And then disappeared, leaving the closet reflected behind me. My changed appearance had been shocking, should, I thought, still be. But it wasn't. Breastless, hairless, with little fat, except around strangely chubby wrists and ankles, no biceps. Aqua crystal eyes. And shorter, I was sure of it. An alien child.

Me. I see me.

My heart, my eyes—both lived in the room next door. Outside my window—no sign of Brinkley's rainbow.

To the desk, the legal pad—one page left. There remained some torn-up pieces of paper under the bed, but that was all. I stared at that last page, eye to a gun barrel, waiting for the trigger pull.

If someone is in the next room, but they stop writing notes to you, do they still exist? Do you?

A chorus of angels spoke their harmonies ever louder: *Velvet, open your eyes* (my mother), *Good morning, how are you today? And how are you, Velvet?* (a male voice), *Isn't the sunshine gorgeous?* (a female voice). There was no static, only clear bell tones. A turned-up radio dial: the volume surged to the level of reverberating eardrums. I thought of what my neighbour had written: all the voices in his room were gone. I wished for silence, the quiet that might mean a chaise lounge in the Elysian Fields next to Brinkley.

V: Please answer me! What's happening?

B: My mother is gone. She smiled, like I have never seen her smile, and then she disappeared. Sensation beneath my bellybutton growing stronger—someone peeling an apple inside me. Apple in my centre turning faster and faster—unloosing its peel in a tingling spiral.

V: Pointless to plead but—Don't go don't go don't go don't go don't go! I don't want to be alone here. And I want to meet you! You know everything about me. Put your hand against the grate and I'll put mine there too.

B: And you know everything about me. Did you feel my hand? I felt yours—my fingers started to tingle. Now both hands are electric. And my scalp feels as though it's sprouting wires. Light is dimming inside. Outside the window—it glows on.

V: Let's sing a song.

B: We can't hear each other.

V: Doesn't matter. I'll know you're singing.

B: What shall we sing?

V: How about "Moon River"?

B: Perfect. Now?

V: Yes.

INT. VELVET'S DELPHI ROOM—TIMELESS

Velvet stands in front of her mirror singing "Moon River."

INT. BRINKLEY'S DELPHI ROOM—TIMELESS

Brinkley stands in front of his mirror singing "Moon River."

V: I think I felt your hand on the grate. There's a warm spot on my palm.

B: Mirror is rippling, a pool, a wishing well. Circles within circles—on and on. I am wishing for your face. Writing this by the glow of the colours outside. Light inside gone. Struck by absence of terror. Calm and clear. Tingling and hot everywhere. Spinning pulse in my centre.

V: Hold my hand in your mind as you go.

B: Velvet—I am leaving. Can scarcely hold pen. Window and bars gone—entering tube. I'll be seeing you . . .

V: Brinkley?

V: Brinkley?

V: Brinkley?

Hands and mouth pressed to the grate—a creature's night-cry. Mouth-mash, bloody lips. Frayed my throat with banshee cries, coughed blood. Eyes salted and burned, lungs wrung. Rocked, rocked, rocked—a madwoman's comfort. Rolled onto my side, in a baby's curl, dulled and stilled. After a while, the body can't keep up with the shriek of the heart.

Out into the bright-as-ever light in my room and over to my desk, pen in hand. Took out the legal pad-with-one-page-left. Sat down and started to write.

Dear Brinkley,

This is the last piece of paper in my room, and when I have filled it with words, I don't know what I will do. I suppose I could write on the walls, but with no one to read my story, I'm not much inclined. My pen moves so slowly now, because I'm afraid of what will happen—or not happen—when I stop writing. It is nothingness we fear, isn't it? But in this place of nothing—here you were. Life finds its way into the oddest corners.

What can I say? You were the best next-door coma neighbour a gal could have. So unexpected are life's shapes, colours and textures, twists and turns, magic tricks and sleights of hand—even to me, a haunted girl of broken faith, a girl who stood in a bathroom and threw up her hands.

I can't die yet, Brinkley. I haven't been given colours, my window hasn't been opened. Maybe those who take themselves out of the game with a belt and a bad makeover feel compelled to return to square one. I don't think I want to die yet, even though I want badly to meet you. If I am given the choice to go back, back into the life I kept messing up—I think I'll take another crack at it. A lot of it sucked, true. But since you had the courage to face down the Shadowman, I think I want to try. I want to do what you did—punch him hard in the face.

Thanks for being my friend. You're right: we are different from most people. But having met you, and knowing that you see what I see, and I see what you see . . . well, you make me feel braver. Brave enough to try life again, if I'm given the chance.

I will carry you with me, Brinkley, if I go back. While I'm busy writing my novella, serving curries and reorganizing my closet, I'll be dreaming of meeting up with you after I'm done with this life, in a Heavenly swimming pool worthy of our favourite movie stars, floating mattress and margarita included.

So the guy I love went off into the sunset, just like in the movies.

Sincerely, Velvet

At the grate, I pressed my mouth to the letter for a long time. Watching it disappear into the wall, my heart squeezed and released, an opening flower. There. It was done.

I stayed and stared and stared, even though I knew no note was coming.

When I began to wonder why it was so dark, I realized I had my eyes closed. On opening them I saw the underside of the bed—I was lying on my back, arms and legs spread mid-snow angel, with no immediate recollection of how I got there. My limbs were awkwardly attached dead weights: turning over was like hauling coils of rope. No letter from Brinkley. Pressed my hands to my eyes and rolled into the light.

I wondered if Brinkley would get a *Children of Divorce* mouse pad in Heaven. I decided that he would.

The room was as changeless as ever, undisturbed by emotion or need: bed, desk, chair, closet, Chinese screen, door, mirror—all constant and faceless as the moon. White, too, was a constant beyond the window, white and more white, full of pain caused by the absence of celestial bodies burning in their own dust, reminding you of home.

My hanging self was gone from the mirror. There stood my alien, baby-headed self, beseeching my oracle with the eyes of a Dickensian street urchin from Mars. How many times in all my life had I stood before a mirror in supplication, hoping that the sage I thought possibly lived behind my eyes would spell an answer on my forehead?

**INT. MIRROR—VELVET'S DELPHI ROOM—
VELVET'S APARTMENT—BATHROOM—TIMELESS**

Velvet stands in her bathroom, face to the mirror. The glass reflects her faithfully: red dress, hacked-off hair, painted face—a weird, drag queen majesty. Her eyes, though fixed on her image, see nothing; or rather they have gone away and see only something hidden, a hermetic reverie. Her movements are slow and floaty, as through water, leaving a wake of chiffon. When she ties a long belt around her neck, it gives her a hapless, S&M look: the woman who spent too much time dressing wrongly for the fetish party.

A boldness now, an ascension: up onto the toilet, fastening the belt to the pipes. Eyes starward, a breath in and out. Step off!

Her feet in their cunning heels appear pointed—ballerina toes—and this, combined with the slight swaying of her hanging body, gives a quaint lyrical effect. The Shadowman, handsome in black cashmere, enters. He unties the belt from Velvet's throat, cradles her in his arms and places her on the floor. He stands up, looks straight ahead. His image flashes from the handsome man in black cashmere to the Zorro look-alike, the Gene Kelly look-alike, the white-faced devil and a drag queen. The drag queen shrugs, and walks out of frame.

Velvet opens her eyes. She does not seem surprised that she is lying on the floor; rather she sits up and looks around, placid as a Buddha, as though this were the natural course of events.

As she stands she smoothes her dress, shakes free the wrinkles.

INT. VELVET'S DELPHI ROOM—CONTINUOUS

I stand before my mirror watching my image, the image of my memories, stand in her bathroom, and wait to see what she will do next. She only stares back at me, eyes wide. I step closer—so does she. I stop, heart pounding out its blood-riddle. I raise a hand—so does she. I lower it—so does she. My eyes shift from the mirror to my own body. And then I see—I am my familiar. My red dress hugs my hips; my feet are squeezed in fancy shoes. My gaze darts back to the mirror. There I remain, though the bathroom is gone and *The Delphi Room* is reflected faithfully. I lift my hands to my hair, my messy Louise Brooks bob. It is soft. Touch my mouth, the red mouth I took so much trouble over. I step to the mirror, raise my hand. Touch, palm to palm. And smile, for here I am: a woman, not too tall, with a rounded, dimpled body and bright eyes. Behind me, in the closet, hangs the pink dress, my temporary *Delphi Room* costume.

I turn from the mirror. The door to my room stands ajar. My insides backflip.

I touch the bed.
I touch the desk.
I touch the chair.
I touch the Chinese screen.
I touch the pink dress.
I touch the window.
I touch the mirror.
I hug Paddington Bear.
I straighten my spine.
I breathe in and out.
I open the door—

The heart does not stop.

About the Author

About the Author

Melia McClure was born in Vancouver. Her fiction has been shortlisted in the Canadian Broadcasting Corporation National Literary Awards. She is also the editor of *Meditation & Health* magazine.

Acknowledgements

The genesis of *The Delphi Room* and its journey into the world owe a great debt of gratitude to many.

I am awed and humbled by the work of the passionate souls at ChiZine Publications: A resounding thank you to the brilliant and courageous Brett Savory and Sandra Kasturi; to my sublime editor Samantha Beiko for her outstanding guidance and generous, effervescent spirit; and to Erik Mohr, for creating book cover perfection. Huge thanks also to Danny Evarts and Klaudia Bednarczyk.

Deep gratitude to Caroline Adderson, whose early encouragement and guidance were, and are, cherished gifts.

To Nancy Richler, whose keen eye and immensely kind shepherding made all the difference, I offer a heartfelt merci.

Warm thanks to Annabel Lyon for valuable insight into an early draft.

To Betsy Warland, for her tremendous kindness, I offer my appreciation.

A grateful salute to Ron Eckel and Suzanne Brandreth at The Cooke Agency International.

Much hat tipping to Cathie Borrie for solace at the W and more.

A loving wink to Karen Schlote for constant "laotong" inspiration.

Immense love to family and friends for unwavering faith, grace and generosity expressed in myriad ways.

And to The Writer's Studio at Simon Fraser University, I extend my gratitude for formative support.

EMB
RACE
THE
ODD

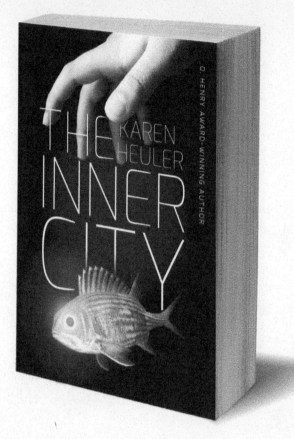

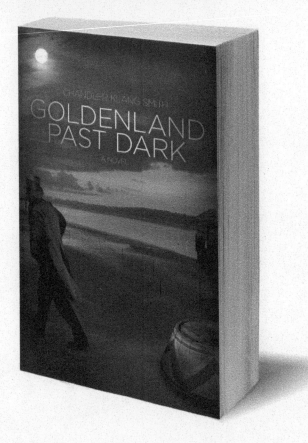

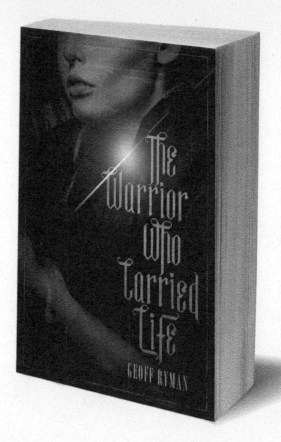

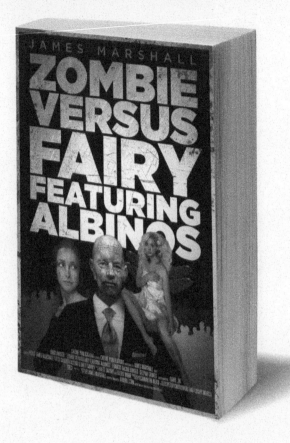

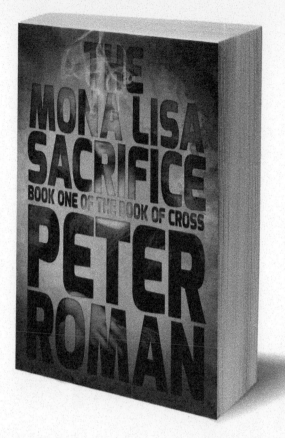

THE 'GEISTERS

DAVID NICKLE

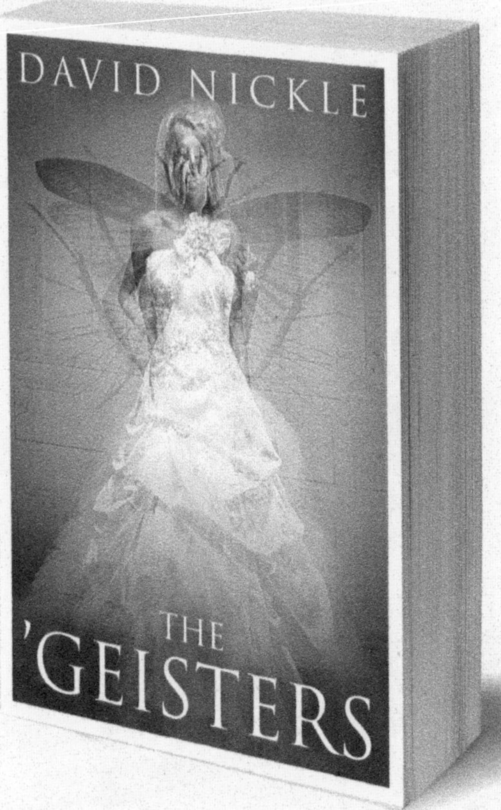

When Ann LeSage was a little girl, she had an invisible friend—a poltergeist, that spoke to her with flying knives and howling winds. She called it the Insect. And with a little professional help, she contained it. But the nightmare never truly ended. As Ann grew from girl into young woman, the Insect grew with her, becoming a thing of murder. Now, as she embarks on a new life married to successful young lawyer Michael Voors, Ann believes that she finally has the Insect under control. But there are others vying to take that control away from her. They may not know exactly what they're dealing with, but they know they want it. They are the 'Geisters. And in pursuing their own perverse dream, they risk spawning the most terrible nightmare of all.

AVAILABLE NOW

978-1-77148-143-4

ALSO AVAILABLE FROM CHIZINE PUBLICATIONS

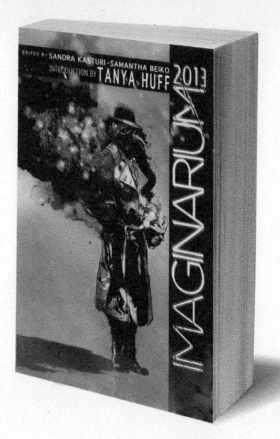

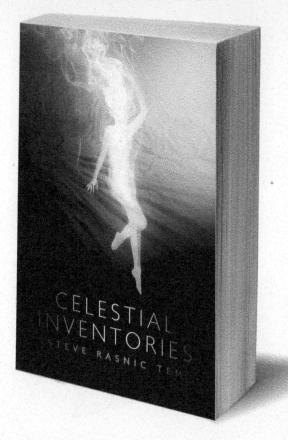

TELL MY SORROWS TO THE STONES

CHRISTOPHER GOLDEN

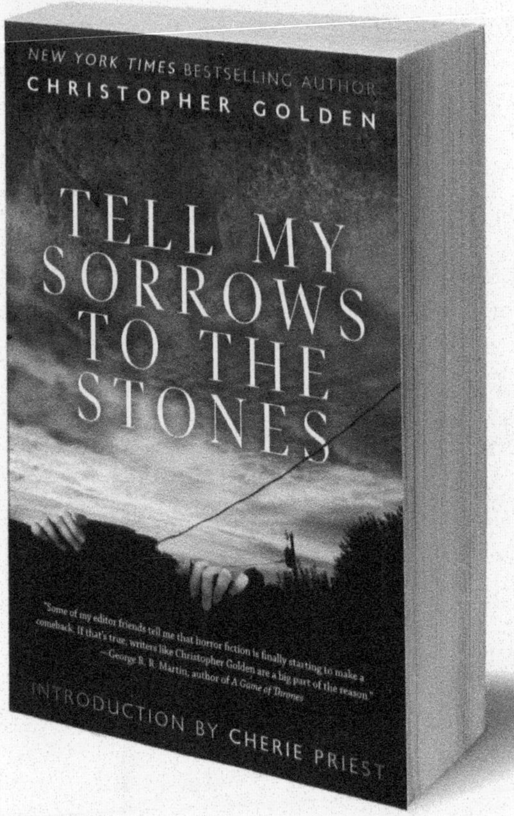

A circus clown willing to give anything to be funny. A spectral gunslinger who must teach a young boy to defend the ones he loves. A lonely widower making a farewell tour of the places that meant the world to his late wife. A faded Hollywood actress out to deprive her ex-husband of his prize possession. A grieving mother who will wait by the railroad tracks for a ghostly train that always has room for one more. A young West Virginia miner whose only hope of survival is a bedtime story. These are just some of the characters to be found in *Tell My Sorrows to the Stones*.

AVAILABLE AUGUST 2013

978-1-77148-153-3

MORE FROM CHIZINE

HORROR STORY AND OTHER HORROR STORIES ROBERT BOYCZUK [978-0-9809410-3-6]

NEXUS: ASCENSION ROBERT BOYCZUK [978-0-9813746-8-0]

THE BOOK OF THOMAS: HEAVEN ROBERT BOYCZUK [978-1-927469-27-9]

PEOPLE LIVE STILL IN CASHTOWN CORNERS TONY BURGESS [978-1-926851-05-1]

THE STEEL SERAGLIO MIKE CAREY, LINDA CAREY & LOUISE CAREY [978-1-926851-53-2]

SARAH COURT CRAIG DAVIDSON [978-1-926851-00-6]

A BOOK OF TONGUES GEMMA FILES [978-0-9812978-6-6]

A ROPE OF THORNS GEMMA FILES [978-1-926851-14-3]

A TREE OF BONES GEMMA FILES [978-1-926851-57-0]

ISLES OF THE FORSAKEN CAROLYN IVES GILMAN [978-1-926851-36-5]

ISON OF THE ISLES CAROLYN IVES GILMAN [978-1-926851-56-3]

FILARIA BRENT HAYWARD [978-0-9809410-1-2]

THE FECUND'S MELANCHOLY DAUGHTER BRENT HAYWARD [978-1-926851-13-6]

IMAGINARIUM 2012: THE BEST CANADIAN SPECULATIVE WRITING
EDITED BY SANDRA KASTURI & HALLI VILLEGAS [978-0-926851-67-9]

CHASING THE DRAGON NICHOLAS KAUFMANN [978-0-9812978-4-2]

OBJECTS OF WORSHIP CLAUDE LALUMIÈRE [978-0-9812978-2-8]

THE DOOR TO LOST PAGES CLAUDE LALUMIÈRE [978-1-926851-12-9]

THE THIEF OF BROKEN TOYS TIM LEBBON [978-0-9812978-9-7]

KATJA FROM THE PUNK BAND SIMON LOGAN [978-0-9812978-7-3]

BULLETTIME NICK MAMATAS [978-1-926851-71-6]

SHOEBOX TRAIN WRECK JOHN MANTOOTH [978-1-926851-54-9]

HAIR SIDE, FLESH SIDE HELEN MARSHALL [978-1-927469-24-8]

NINJA VERSUS PIRATE FEATURING ZOMBIES JAMES MARSHALL [978-1-926851-58-7]

PICKING UP THE GHOST TONE MILAZZO [978-1-926851-35-8]

BEARDED WOMEN TERESA MILBRODT [978-1-926851-46-4]

NAPIER'S BONES DERRYL MURPHY [978-1-926851-09-9]

MONSTROUS AFFECTIONS DAVID NICKLE [978-0-9812978-3-5]

EUTOPIA DAVID NICKLE [978-1-926851-11-2]

RASPUTIN'S BASTARDS DAVID NICKLE [978-1-926851-59-4]

CITIES OF NIGHT PHILIP NUTMAN [978-0-9812978-8-0]

JANUS JOHN PARK [978-1-927469-10-1]

EVERY SHALLOW CUT TOM PICCIRILLI [978-1-926851-10-5]

BRIARPATCH TIM PRATT [978-1-926851-44-0]

THE CHOIR BOATS DANIEL A. RABUZZI [978-0-980941-07-4]

THE INDIGO PHEASANT DANIEL A. RABUZZI [978-1-927469-09-5]

EVERY HOUSE IS HAUNTED IAN ROGERS [978-1-927469-16-3]

ENTER, NIGHT MICHAEL ROWE [978-1-926851-45-7]

REMEMBER WHY YOU FEAR ME ROBERT SHEARMAN [978-1-927469-21-7]

CHIMERASCOPE DOUGLAS SMITH [978-0-9812978-5-9]

THE PATTERN SCARS CAITLIN SWEET [978-1-926851-43-3]

THE TEL AVIV DOSSIER LAVIE TIDHAR AND NIR YANIV [978-0-9809410-5-0]

IN THE MEAN TIME PAUL TREMBLAY [978-1-926851-06-8]

SWALLOWING A DONKEY'S EYE PAUL TREMBLAY [978-1-926851-69-3]

THE HAIR WREATH AND OTHER STORIES HALLI VILLEGAS [978-1-926851-02-0]

THE WORLD MORE FULL OF WEEPING ROBERT J. WIERSEMA [978-0-9809410-9-8]

WESTLAKE SOUL RIO YOUERS [978-1-926851-55-6]

MAJOR KARNAGE GORD ZAJAC [978-0-9813746-6-6]

"IF YOUR TASTE IN FICTION RUNS TO THE DISTURBING, DARK, AND AT LEAST PARTIALLY WEIRD, CHANCES ARE YOU'VE HEARD OF CHIZINE PUBLICATIONS—CZP—A YOUNG IMPRINT THAT IS NONETHELESS PRODUCING STARTLINGLY BEAUTIFUL BOOKS OF STARKLY, DARKLY LITERARY QUALITY."

—DAVID MIDDLETON, *JANUARY MAGAZINE*

ALSO AVAILABLE FROM CHIZINE PUBLICATIONS